MURDER AT THE OLYMPICS
A 1920S COZY HISTORICAL MYSTERY

A GINGER GOLD MYSTERY
BOOK TWENTY-FIVE

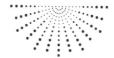

LEE STRAUSS

Murder at the Olympics

Copyright © 2024 by Lee Strauss

Cover by Jordan Strauss

Illustration by Tasia Strauss

All rights reserved.

No part of this book may be reproduced in any form or by any electronic or mechanical means, including information storage and retrieval systems, without written permission from the author, except for the use of brief quotations in a book review.

Library and Archives Canada Cataloguing in Publication

Title: Murder at the Olympics / Lee Strauss.

Names: Strauss, Lee (Novelist), author.

Series: Strauss, Lee (Novelist). Ginger Gold mystery ; 25.

Description: Series statement: A Ginger Gold mystery ; 25 | "A 1920s cozy historical mystery."

Identifiers: Canadiana (print) 20230587372 | Canadiana (ebook) 20230587380 | ISBN 9781774094396 (hardcover) | ISBN 9781774094365 (softcover) | ISBN 9781774094389 (Kindle) | ISBN 9781774094402 (EPUB)

Classification: LCC PS8637.T739 M8738 2024 | DDC C813/.6—dc23

GINGER GOLD MYSTERIES
(IN ORDER)

Murder on the SS *Rosa*
Murder at Hartigan House
Murder at Bray Manor
Murder at Feathers & Flair
Murder at the Mortuary
Murder at Kensington Gardens
Murder at St. George's Church
The Wedding of Ginger & Basil
Murder Aboard the Flying Scotsman
Murder at the Boat Club
Murder on Eaton Square
Murder by Plum Pudding
Murder on Fleet Street
Murder at Brighton Beach
Murder in Hyde Park
Murder at the Royal Albert Hall
Murder in Belgravia

Murder on Mallowan Court
Murder at the Savoy
Murder at the Circus
Murder at the Boxing Club
Murder in France
Murder at Yuletide
Murder at Madame Tussauds
Murder at St. Paul's Cathedral
Murder at the Olympics

NOTES FROM THE AUTHOR

Whenever a story is set in a real place and time, especially depicting a documented event, choices need to be made as to what parts need to stay true to history and what parts can be embellished or invented.

The 1928 Summer Olympics is one of those events. In *Murder at the Olympics* I tried to stay true to the description of the stadium and the city of Amsterdam at the time. I did take liberties in placing the stables closer to the Olympic Stadium in this fictional account.

I've included real personalities with those I've created. Real persons include Alice Milliat and various athletes. I've given a fictional character the privilege of winning an equestrian event that was in reality won by another.

MURDER AT THE OLYMPICS

CHAPTER ONE

Clive Pippins stood at the window of his attic bedroom in Hartigan House, aware only of the ache in his knees, the pinch in his back, and the crick in his neck. An old man stared back at him from the reflection in the glass. Pippins blinked back. That poor fellow was as bald as a billiard ball, with droopy skin on his long face. Watery blue eyes squinted in the sunlight, nearly disappearing behind skin folds. Though tall and lean, the man's shoulders fell forward, creating a roundness in his upper spine. Pippins empathised with the bloke, feeling the pain in his own neck in much the same place.

Pippins became aware of the warmth in the room, and the green, leafy trees outside reminded him it was the middle of summer. One must open the windows and allow for a breeze in such instances. Of this, he was fairly certain. Unlatching the casement, he pushed the glass open like a small barn door, and peered out.

In the garden—and it was such a beautiful garden. Who was responsible for that?—Pippins saw the man trimming the bushes. Clarence? Was it? Or Clem? Clements, yes, that was his name.

A boy sat on a patio chair holding a little black-and-white dog. Scout and Boss. Pippins exhaled. Yes, he remembered.

A man joined the boy and gestured to the door. It was clear he wanted the lad and the dog to go inside. Pippins sensed that something important was happening that day. There were so many things to remember. He pinched his eyes together as he tried to draw it up. How could he remember the state of the butler's pantry, where every bottle and jar was placed, every piece of silver, but he couldn't remember yesterday?

His vision blurred when he reopened his eyes. Blinking back the dratted tears—why did his eyes water so much?—he stared at the people in the garden below. A red-headed little girl held a doll, her father crouching as he spoke to the child. Poor thing was in tears.

Now Pippins remembered. Mr. Hartigan was taking the little miss to America.

Pippins knew he'd better hurry and hobbled down that long set of narrow stairs in time to say goodbye. If only his blasted knees didn't hurt so much.

CHAPTER TWO

Hartigan House was a three-storey limestone residence in London's prestigious South Kensington district. The place had a sense of stillness and quiet that its owner, Mrs. Ginger Reed, found unsettling. Her discomfort wasn't as intense now as when she'd arrived five years earlier to claim her inheritance. *Oh mercy, how time has flown by!*

The Mallowan Court house had sat empty for ten years. It had taken several weeks, even months, to freshen the old girl up with new paint, wallpaper, and décor fitting with the style-moderne trends of the day.

Pippins had come with the house. Her beloved butler had been old then, already many years older than the average life expectancy, even in the new century. He was in his mid-seventies, and Ginger had finally convinced him to retire, though he insisted on keeping the attic bedroom. The climb up and down the staircase, he claimed, was responsible for his extended years.

The sitting room was Ginger's favourite. Not only did she love the warm-yellow, velvet settee and matching armchairs that sat next to the stone fireplace, the rich red Turkish carpet on the wooden floor, and the long window that let in the summer sunlight, she especially admired the Waterhouse painting of *The Mermaid* above the mantel. It was an exquisite piece of art and had enormous sentimental value. The painting had been a gift to her mother from her father, and Ginger had been told the red-headed siren had an uncanny resemblance to her mother, who had sadly passed away soon after Ginger herself was born.

Ginger had dressed in a simple cotton day frock, with a decorative band at the low waist, matching summer jacket, and plain white low-heeled pumps. Perfectly suitable for travelling. As she sat in one of the armchairs, Boss, her Boston terrier, jumped onto her lap and curled up, tucking himself against her abdomen. He, too, was getting on in years, having slowed down to where he no longer begged to come along for rides with her in the motorcar. *It's a good thing this time*, Ginger mused, as there was no way she could take him to where she, Basil, and their son, Scout, were about to go—Amsterdam and the Games of the IX Olympiad!

Ginger had had little exposure to the Dutch language, though she had mastered German and

French through her studies at Boston University and her time spent in the war. When she'd expressed her concern about language difficulties, Basil surprised her by saying he could speak Dutch. "Enough to get by, love." Apparently, Amsterdam had been a favourite holiday destination for the Reed family.

The dowager Lady Ambrosia Gold sat on the settee opposite Ginger. After what she described as a frightful lapse in judgement, her grey hair had grown out of the shorter bob—which, according to Ginger, had placed at least one of the dowager's feet into the twentieth century. It was now pinned in a small bun on the top of her head. She sat upright in the manner that would suggest a good corset, the lace collar of her starched blouse reaching the sagging jowls of her jawline.

Ambrosia carried herself with the air of someone who understood privilege and her place in British peerage. She, like Boss, was advanced in years and could thank her social status and good genetics for her extended time on earth, as well as her natural obstinance to refuse to let go of this life.

"I imagine you'll see Felicia," she said with a sniff.

Felicia Gold, now Lady Davenport-Witt, the granddaughter and only living blood relative of the dowager, had moved with her husband to Amsterdam a month earlier, claiming that a home on the Continent was more convenient for travel, which she and her husband Charles had decided, rather suddenly, to do. Ginger wondered if this was their answer to easing a troubled marriage, and if so, she hoped it was working.

Ambrosia wasn't that forgiving. She'd ranted for days after Felicia and Charles left, saying that Felicia had always been a difficult and selfish child. "I'm far too easy on my grandchild," the dowager was known to say. But how could Ambrosia be to blame for her grievances? If her son and daughter-in-law hadn't died in that carriage crash, Ambrosia would never have had to bring up two more children. One child, she'd proclaimed about her son Robert, was enough. And, one mustn't forget, Ambrosia had been on her own, a widow herself already.

"Yes," Ginger said, answering the dowager. "From what I can tell from her letters, she's very excited about witnessing the Games. Surely, she has written to you?"

Ambrosia's gaze moved to the window and a view of Mallowan Court and Felicia's empty house across the way.

"My eyesight isn't what it used to be," Ambrosia said with a flick of her veiny hands, her bony fingers adorned with rings with large baubles. "Langley reads them to me, but perhaps I dozed off at that part."

Ginger doubted that. If anything, Ambrosia would be extra attentive to any news that came from her granddaughter. The dowager could express no pleasure in Felicia's life choices, even if they brought Felicia happiness . . . if such choices took Felicia from London.

The door to the sitting room pushed open, and

Scout stepped in. "Oh, there you are. Dad says the taxicab will be here in ten minutes."

Ginger smiled at her adopted son. Once a street orphan, Scout was quickly turning into a handsome young man. His blond hair had darkened and, with the help of hair oil, no longer stood up, untamed in every direction. He'd always been small for his age, and though this would be a bothersome feature for other fourteen-year-old boys, Scout embraced his size, a positive attribute for the jockey he was determined to become. He was home from his special equestrian-focused boarding school for the summer. He was thrilled to attend the Olympics, especially since Ginger had pulled strings and got him a position in the stables at the Olympic grounds, grooming the horses.

Seeing Scout, Boss jumped off Ginger's lap and went to the lad. Scout, seated in an armchair, reached his hand out to the dog. Boss licked Scout's hand but didn't move to climb into his arms. Scout picked him up instead.

Ginger's heart warmed, her mind going back to when she and Boss first met Scout. He had still been missing a front tooth and dropped his H's in a pure cockney fashion. Scout had cared for Boss in the third-class deck of the SS *Rosa,* where the animals were kept, and had become fast friends with the dog.

"Are we ready?"

Basil, Ginger's husband and a chief inspector at Scotland Yard, joined them in the sitting room. Ginger smiled inwardly as she stared up at him, always in admiration, not only of his stalwart character but his hazel eyes, which became more handsome, it seemed, by the advancing crow's feet and the greying of his temples.

"The taxicab is here," he announced.

Ginger rubbed Boss' ears, saying goodbye before Scout set him on the floor. She went to Ambrosia. "Don't get up, Grandmama." She kissed the family matron on a soft crêpe-like cheek. "We'll be back in less than two weeks."

Ambrosia didn't smile. Not long ago, she would've insisted on joining in the fun, but these days, she didn't want to be away from her own comforts.

"I'll bring you back a souvenir," Ginger said.

"Unless that souvenir is Felicia," Ambrosia grumbled, "I don't want it."

Oh, poor thing! Ginger thought. *I really must convince Felicia to come back to London for a visit soon.*

Pippins and Nanny Green waited at the front door, Pips holding Ginger's gloves and Nanny Green holding Ginger's wriggling year-and-a-half-old daughter Rosa. Ginger swooped Rosa into her arms and kissed her on the head. "I'll miss you, little one! Be good for Nanny." Ginger handed Rosa to Basil, who swung his little daughter in the air, much to the child's delight, producing a round of delightful giggling.

Basil handed Rosa to the nanny, and Ginger watched dolefully as the two of them made their way up the curving staircase. High above their heads hung an enormous electric chandelier, which, when turned on, lit the black and white tiles of the entranceway with its sparkling reflection.

"Where's Digby?" Ginger asked, turning her attention to Pippins. Digby was the younger replacement butler.

"It's his day off, madam," Pippins said. Ginger's beloved retired butler considered her with his deep cornflower-blue eyes. Another ageing resident of Hartigan House, he'd long ago lost his hair, but Ginger noted he was also losing his height, his shoulders and neck moving incrementally forward. "It's my pleasure to see you on your way."

Ginger wanted to escort the man to a chair and insist he rest.

"Thank you, Pips," Ginger said as she accepted her gloves and put them on. "I trust you to ensure everything runs smoothly while we're gone. Should something of concern arise, I've left our hotel's address and telephone number on the desk in my study."

"Of course, madam. You and Lord Gold have a lovely time away."

Ginger shot Basil a look of alarm. Daniel, Lord Gold, had been her first husband, now dead for almost ten years.

CHAPTER THREE

After a night at a hotel in Harwich, they sailed across the southwestern tip of the North Sea, Ginger and Basil standing shoulder to shoulder on the open-air passenger deck. The mid-summer wind was brisk enough that Ginger's hand often moved to her hat to ensure it didn't blow off her head.

"I'm worried about Pippins."

Basil nodded. "He seems to have lost his footing lately."

"It's come on so quickly," she added with regret, "or have I been too busy to notice?"

Basil reached for her hand. "I think Pippins has been very good at masquerading."

"I feel dreadful about making him stay in the attic with all those steps. He insists they're fine, but I've seen him wince in pain when he didn't know I was looking."

"Can't you give him one of the empty rooms on our

floor?" Basil asked, then as if catching himself added, "No, I suppose not."

There was no way propriety would allow the dowager Lady Gold to sleep on the same floor as a household staff member. However, Ginger had an idea. Perhaps they could set him up at Witt House. She'd ask Felicia about it when she saw her former sister-in-law in Amsterdam.

Her attention was caught by Scout, who lingered further down the deck. He leaned against the rail, his gaze moving from the horizon to a pretty girl wearing a checked, wide-collared day frock, sitting in one of the nearby chairs. A matching large bow held back her shoulder-length hair.

Ginger let out a wistful sigh. Her little boy was growing up.

Basil gently squeezed Ginger's hand. "Is everything all right?"

"Everything is utterly wonderful, love," Ginger said. "Being on this ferry reminds me of when we met on our journey from America." The ferry was notably smaller than the steamship they'd travelled on, However, being out on a large body of water with no landmass in sight evoked similar emotions. "Can you believe it's been five years this month?"

Basil's smile widened. "The best five years of my life."

Ginger laughed. "You didn't think that way originally. If I recall, your first impressions of me were rather different."

"You could say the same thing about me."

Ginger pressed her shoulder into Basil's arm playfully. "I wasn't about to arrest you."

"You *were* rather annoying," Basil teased back. "Trying to do my job for me."

"I don't think much has changed in that regard." Ginger glanced at Scout, who'd subtly moved closer to the girl he seemed to fancy. "And Scout was just a small lad. Look at him. Lovestruck already."

Basil followed Ginger's gaze, his smile wavering. "I suppose I'll have to chat with him soon on how to treat a lady of interest properly."

"I believe so," Ginger said. "With him away at school, we don't see how fast he's changing. Before we know it, he's going to be a man."

"There must be a way to slow time down," Basil said. "A button to push somewhere."

Ginger's mind went to Ambrosia and her little dog, Boss. Five years didn't just change the young. "I'd certainly like to know about such a button."

"Excuse me." A stout man with a short moustache and wearing a blue suit and a straw hat, approached them with the confidence of one used to interrupting private conversations. "Madam, are you Mrs. Reed, the former Lady Gold?"

A reporter, Ginger guessed. Not surprising that members of the press would be heading toward the site of the summer games. "Yes, I am," Ginger answered politely. "And you are?"

"Ernest Bottomley with *The Daily Picture*." He chuckled. "I recognised you from, er, the society pages. Not my beat, yer know, which is why I've never seen you publicly before. I confess, I never pictured you as a redhead."

Ginger shared a glance with Basil, who was clearly scowling. *The Daily Picture* had a reputation for sensationalising, with a lesser emphasis on the truth.

"Yes, well, Mr. Bottomley," Ginger started, "Red, brown, black, blond, we're all one of those few." She couldn't see evidence of Mr. Bottomley's hair or hair colour, so she presumed the man was now bald.

"You are a lady about town," Mr. Bottomley said, not showing any signs of leaving. "A philanthropist, naturally; many ladies of your stature are. But your reputation for solving crimes sets you apart and gets the tongues wagging. Murders, no less!"

"I assure you, I don't work alone." Ginger thought of Magna Jones, her intrepid assistant at the office of Lady Gold Investigations, and, of course, Basil. "You must've heard of my husband . . ." Ginger gripped Basil's arm. "Chief Inspector Basil Reed of Scotland Yard."

Mr. Bottomley nodded rapidly and stretched out a hand in Basil's direction. Basil accepted it and endured a stiff pumping of his wrist. "Of course I have," the reporter said. "It's a pleasure to meet you in person."

Ginger thought the man might politely excuse himself after that, but he settled in against the rail instead. "The two of you are headed to the Olympics, I'm guessing."

"We are," Basil said, then pointed at Scout. "Along with our son."

"He's a jockey in training," Ginger added proudly. "He's assisting with caring for the horses involved in the equestrian events."

"How nice," Mr. Bottomley said quickly, as if he hardly had the patience to wait for Ginger to finish so he could resume his own line of thinking. "Such a shame about our ladies' track and field team."

Ginger raised a brow. "You must now share whatever scandalous information you have, Mr. Bottomley."

"The ladies are all up in arms because of the sudden changes to the track and field programme. Though it's terrific that foot races have been added, the Olympic committee have reduced the previously agreed-upon number of ten to three, and one of those left in the competition is the eight hundred metres!"

"Why on earth would the Olympic committee do that?" Ginger asked. Eight hundred metres was nearly half a mile!

"Apparently, there's a strong consensus that these kinds of physically taxing sports aren't appropriate for the weaker sex."

Ginger was incredulous. "Then why leave in the eight hundred metres?"

Mr. Bottomley shrugged. "To make their point? The British ladies are boycotting the events altogether." The reporter tipped his hat. "I'll go my way now. Didn't mean to disturb your pleasant time aboard." His eyes twinkled with a certain sense of glee.

Ginger pinched her lips. "I hate to say I have to agree with that distasteful little man. It is a shame the British women's track and field team is boycotting the Games." She linked her arm with Basil's and nodded towards their son. Scout had inched closer to the poor unsuspecting girl, whose nose was now deeply into a thick leather-bound book. "We must rescue our son before he embarrasses himself."

"By embarrassing him first?" Basil returned slyly.

Ginger hummed. "I see your point. A conundrum indeed. How do you propose we proceed?"

"I say we appeal to his stomach," Basil said. "There's a restaurant below deck."

"Good idea," Ginger said. "You fetch Scout, and I'll select a table."

CHAPTER FOUR

Ginger, who wasn't fazed by much, felt heady, seated at the Olympic stadium with eager spectators. The anticipation of the onlookers was nearly palpable, as if they were each a living cell of a greater being, breathing as one.

She sat beside Basil and Scout on the long side of the oval in the reserved section, with its covering overhead for shade from the strong end-of-July sun. Opposite them was the entrance, where people streamed into the stadium. The flags of many nations fluttered in the breeze along with banners proudly announcing *Olympische Zomerspelen 1928* or *Spelen van de IXe Olympiade - 28 juli t/m 12 augustus.* Just beyond, the cauldron tower poked into the sky.

There were two empty seats beside Ginger, and her gaze scoured the massive crowd, searching for the familiar faces of Charles and Felicia. They were to meet them there. Except for a few rather short letters, Ginger hadn't communicated with her former sister-in-law since she and Charles had left for the Netherlands, and Ginger was eager to catch up.

While she waited, she took a moment to examine her features in her silver-embossed Armand powder and rouge compact—*such a handy little invention*. With a simple click of a button, the palm-sized disc split open like a clam, one side with a mirror and the other unfolding two separate discs, one with a powder cake and one with rouge. Ginger quickly powdered her nose, a necessity with this heat, but her cheeks were rosy enough because of the same heat. She'd plucked her eyebrows that morning as she did every morning, and they were delightfully thin and well arched. Daylight required only a light touch of make-up—a bit of blue eyeshadow, and a single layer of mascara. She wore a floral-printed scarf over her head, a cooler option than a hat.

"How many people do you think are here, Dad?" Scout asked, his face flushed with excitement.

"I read this stadium was built to hold over thirty-one thousand."

"Thirty-one thousand people?" Scout's eyes rounded with wonder. "That's the same size as a city!"

Ginger shared her son's amazement.

"Fancy meeting you here!" a voice called out.

Ginger turned towards the loud voice and held a blank expression, even as she felt dismay at seeing the ambitious journalist they'd met on the ferry.

"Hello, Mr. Bottomley," she said as she fanned herself gracefully. Basil nodded politely.

"It is a wonder, isn't it," Ginger added, "that we'd be seated near each other in this enormous crowd."

"The committee was convinced to give the press seats under the awning so we could see properly and not have our reporting inconvenienced by the sun's glare. It seems they put the Brits together." Mr. Bottomley pointed to the far end of the covered area. "The Americans are down there. I believe the French and other continental countries are on the other side, and of course, the Dutch are everywhere."

A man in the American seats stared in their direction, glaring. Or was he squinting in the sunlight?

Mr. Bottomley snarled.

"Who is that?" Ginger asked with curiosity.

"Jack Montrose," Mr. Bottomley returned.

"You don't appear to like him."

"We have a history," Mr. Bottomley grunted as if the short comment was explanation enough.

Ginger was happy to be distracted by Felicia and Charles' arrival.

"Just in time!" Ginger said with a smile. She stood and held out her arms. "It's just like you to be late, even for the Olympics!"

"Pish," Felicia said, accepting Ginger's embrace. "The traffic is dreadful. So good to see you!"

Ginger greeted Charles, and Basil extended his hand to the man in welcome. "Amsterdam seems to suit you," he said.

"It's been jolly good," Charles admitted.

Felicia held her husband's arm. "We're having such a great time."

Ginger was pleased. The young couple had had a rough start to their marriage, and Felicia had spent many months feeling unhappy. Seeing the joy on her face now as she smiled up at Charles did Ginger's heart a world of good.

"Hello, Scout," Felicia said. "Are you excited?"

"Very much, Aunt Felicia. Did Mum tell you I'm volunteering to help in the stables?"

"She did tell me in her letters. I'm thrilled for you. Is that where you're staying?"

Scout nodded with a look of glee. "I couldn't be happier."

As Charles chatted with Basil about the weather and polite but mundane topics, Ginger pulled Felicia close. "Ambrosia sends her greetings."

"Oh, I do miss Grandmama," Felicia said. "She's not much of a letter writer."

"She's lost a bit of the skip in her step since you've left," Ginger said, though she kept her voice light. She didn't want to make Felicia feel bad for simply living her life. "When do you think you'll be back in London?"

Felicia shrugged. "I can't really say. You must do your best to keep Grandmama entertained until I return."

"I'll do my best. Later, you must tell me all about your life here." Ginger's attention was caught by activity on the field. "It looks like the ceremony is about to begin."

The loud musical tones of a brass band prevented further conversation, and every person's rapt attention was turned to the field. What followed was the Parade of Nations, a seemingly endless ribbon of athletes proudly wearing their country's colours, with one esteemed member from each team carrying their country's flag.

"Forty-six nations!" Scout said. "That's what it says in the programme. Greece is to go first because they founded the original Olympic games."

"And as the host team, the Dutch are last," Ginger pointed out. "That's new."

Mr. Bottomley, who'd watched the reunion between Ginger and Felicia with subtle interest, muttered from the side of his mouth, loud enough for Ginger to hear. "Can't believe they let the Boche in."

Ginger looked the other way. Sentiment towards the German people had, naturally, soured since the war, and she herself wasn't immune. But they were in a time of peace now. And if wrongs couldn't be completely forgotten, they could be put aside for the next two weeks.

The Olympic Oath followed the parade. The Dutch footballer, Harry Dénis, had been given the honour. Stepping onto the podium, he spoke into the microphone—a new piece of technology that amplified his voice to be heard over the whole stadium.

"We swear that we are taking part in the Olympic Games as loyal competitors, observing the rules governing the Games, and anxious to show a spirit of chivalry, for the honour of our countries and for the glory of sport."

To the delight of the crowd, dancers and gymnasts filled the field.

Mr. Bottomley continued his commentary. "The naysayers want the ladies to stick to the gentler sports. They say the women have no reason to engage in the more strenuous activities." He laid his narrow-eyed gaze on Ginger. "What is your opinion on the matter, Mrs. Reed?"

"On or off the record?" Ginger answered.

The man smiled slyly. "On, preferably."

"Then I withhold comment," Ginger said. "I have no compulsion to be dragged into controversy."

"Very well, off the record."

"Can I trust you, Mr. Bottomley?"

He had the decency to hesitate before lying. "Of course."

"Well, if you must know, I side with women having

a choice. Let them decide what sport they want to participate in. Why should a committee of men have the final say?"

Mr. Bottomley laughed as Basil quietly groaned beside her. So much for staying out of the controversy.

The Netherlands were well represented with the nation's official colour of orange on grand display. The ceremony ended with the introduction of Prince Hendrik, the husband of Queen Wilhelmina, who announced the official opening, which was then followed by a release of doves and the cauldron lighting on top of the Olympic tower.

Scout pointed, his eyes flashing with excitement. "The fire will stay lit for the duration of the games! Wouldn't it be grand if they did that at every Olympiad?"

Ginger agreed. "It would."

Track and field events were scheduled for the next day, and the names of many athletes were bandied about: Jack London of Great Britain, Percy Williams of Canada, and Ray Barbuti from the United States; and for the women, there were Lina Radke of Germany, Betty Robinson from America, and Kinue Hitomi, who was Japan's first female Olympic athlete.

Ginger wasn't athletic in the same way as her friend Haley Higgins was, but she could run if needed. She had done so on more than one occasion during the war. Then, it had been her life on the line or the life of someone she was commissioned to save. Ginger would rather not exert herself in such a manner for any other reason, but she admired those who did it for sport. She was looking forward to the women's 800 metre race in particular, as were hundreds of other onlookers.

CHAPTER FIVE

Excitement followed the games over the next two days. Pomp and hype were featured through the athletic events with exuberant winners and disappointed losers. Emotions ran high when records were broken, including when Mikio Oda of Japan won a gold medal in the triple jump event and became the first athlete from an Asian country to win gold.

By the last day of July, Ginger and Basil had formed the routine of enjoying breakfast in their hotel room, then heading to the stadium by water taxi, where they first called in at stables to see Scout before heading back to the races or whatever athletic event was scheduled.

As Ginger and Basil manoeuvred through the crowds, they couldn't help but bump into people.

"Those pigtails are ridiculous! She should be disqualified based on her fashion sense alone."

Ginger turned to the judgemental voice, surprised to find the bitter words had come from the mouth of another athlete. She remembered seeing the woman's photo from the Olympic brochure: Charlotte Hartley, a pretty American with a modern blond bob.

Soon, Ginger and Basil were sitting under the Olympic stadium awning, feeling rather hot with perspiration. Thankfully, a lad selling Coca-Cola came their way. The American company was a new sponsor of the Games, providing refreshments for the athlete's thirst. Ginger quite enjoyed the bubbly drink, tart yet sweet.

There was much talk amongst the attendees, and Ginger couldn't help but overhear a couple behind her musing about the races.

"It's a shame Alice Milliat won't attend," the lady said.

With a glimpse, Ginger noted the middle-aged woman wearing a large-brimmed hat and frantically fanning herself with the brochure.

Her gentleman companion sniffed. "I say, she's rather caused enough trouble."

"Oh, Maurice! I admire her! The Olympic committee denied female athletes a chance to participate in athletics, so she started her own women's Olympics! Can you imagine? I wish I had her gumption."

"You've got plenty of gumption, Mary," the man said with a hint of exhaustion.

Ginger leaned into Basil and said quietly, "They're talking about Alice Milliat and how she had gumption."

"Oh?" Basil returned, his eyes flickering as if he was trying to recall an earlier conversation.

"You know," Ginger said, "the French rower I told you about who played a significant role in convincing the Olympic committee to add more events for women." Ginger had read about Mademoiselle Milliat extensively. Back in 1912, she'd protested against women being limited to sports that focused on their physical attractiveness. An excessive emphasis had been placed on feminine frailty—and still was, even in these modern times—allocating women to sports like tennis, archery, swimming, golf, and skating.

The attitude was exemplified in a statement Olympics' founder and former president Pierre de Coubertin had made when the Olympic Games were first revived. The games were for "the solemn and periodic exaltation of male athleticism," he wrote, "with female applause as reward." Even though it had been several decades since that preposterous and misogynistic statement, Ginger still found herself irritated by it.

"If you'll recall," Ginger continued, "Alice Milliat planned a women-only competition in protest, which she also called *The Olympics*, much to the original

Olympic organisers' dismay. And to the surprise of many, men mostly, her event was successful."

"She had gumption, indeed," Basil said.

"The Olympic committee agreed to make concessions and allow women to compete here in the first *official* Olympic Games, provided Alice Milliat stopped using the word "Olympics" for her own competition. She agreed to that. But, at the last moment, the Olympic organisers reduced the events for women by half."

"Miss Milliat's reticence to attend is understandable."

"Yes, it is. And the British women are protesting," Ginger said, "because, finally, women are allowed to compete in athletics in the Olympics, but then they're only given three races. One of which many think is extreme and unkind to women."

"Do you think the eight hundred metres is extreme and unkind?" Basil said. "It does seem rather a hard event, even for men."

"If a woman wants to train for such exertion, if she thinks she can do it, then yes, I believe it should be permitted. We'll see the results of the experiment soon enough." Ginger finished her bottle of Coca-Cola and set it aside. "The race will continue, and someone will win. Perhaps a Brit, after all."

Basil raised a brow. "How so?"

"According to the latest news on the race, one

British female athlete is resisting the boycott. A Miss Nora Graves. She's competing as an independent."

"I've heard the name," Basil said. "She's a strong contender."

"Perhaps Miss Graves sees things the way we do."

The men's 100 and 200 metre races were the next to run. Using the field glasses she carried in her handbag, Ginger spotted Mr. Bottomley with a pack of photographers on the edge of the track near the start line; his pencil gripped tightly by thick fingers. Other journalists and photographers positioned themselves along the halfway points, with more at the finish line. Other men stood, hat brims shading serious faces, with notebooks in hand, ready to write their stories. Canadian underdog Williams surprised everyone by winning both.

"It's Canada's lucky day," Basil said.

The women's 100 metres was next. Checking her programme, Ginger read the competitors' names, thirty-one in all, although many of them hadn't made it through to today's final.

With a long red fingernail, Ginger poked at the photo of the woman who didn't like pigtails. *Charlotte Hartley, that was her name.* She and Betty Robinson—only sixteen years old—represented the USA. Nora Graves was listed as independent and was notable for the short pigtails she chose to wear.

Ginger always rooted for the country of her birth and current home, Britain, when they were represented, but she also quietly cheered for America, where she spent her formative years and where her half-sister had been born and still resided. The dynamic between Miss Hartley and Miss Graves felt personal to Ginger.

Their coaches instructed both women before the girls headed for their starting positions. Ginger paid close attention to the faces of Miss Graves and the British coach—according to the programme, his name was Mr. Claude Dankworth. Miss Graves looked familiar to Ginger, though she couldn't put her finger on why. And she was certain she'd never had the pleasure of meeting the rogue athlete before.

The coach had an intense expression, his hands in tight fists at his side. Miss Graves pointed her finger, her face tightening around her lips. Clearly, there was no love lost between the two. Ginger's natural curiosity was piqued, but she stopped herself from making assumptions. It wasn't uncommon for emotions to get away during high-pressured events such as the Olympic Games.

A whistle blew, and the athletes stepped onto the track.

Miss Hartley moved towards her position next to Miss Graves. *Wait. Did the American just knock into the British athlete?* Through her field glasses, Ginger saw Miss Graves scowl over her shoulder, but if a foul had been committed, none of the judges spotted it.

Ginger jumped to her feet at the quickly run race and cheered as America's Betty Robinson broke a world record in the 100 metre race. The silver and gold medals went to Canadians Fanny Rosenfeld and Ethel Smith. It was truly a great day for Canada.

And tomorrow would be the heats for the women's 800 metre race. Already shrouded in controversy, the race would be a spectacle to witness. Ginger had known the Olympics would be exciting, and she wasn't wrong.

CHAPTER SIX

Ginger and Basil had spent a day watching the swimming competitions—a nice change of venue and discipline. However, the highly anticipated day of the women's 800 metre race, which had been on everyone's minds, was finally here. As always, Felicia and Charles arrived late, flushed, happy, and just in time.

The 800 metre race had already been run by the men, with Britain's Douglas Lowe winning the Gold, an exciting race!

Today was the women's turn.

"This is so thrilling," Felicia said. "That brave woman, Miss Graves, running without the support of her teammates. Or is she brave? I suppose her teammates would disagree. Perhaps she's just silly."

"It would depend on who you talk to," Ginger said, thinking Miss Graves might be both brave and silly.

"Mr. Bottomley might have a different view from Mr. Montrose."

"Ah yes," Felicia returned, "that journalist from New York. His pieces are rather negative, at least the ones I've read." She turned to her husband. "Wouldn't you agree, darling?"

"Indeed," Charles said. "His saltiness sells papers."

The stadium buzzed with anticipation and wonder: how would the female athletes fare with such a rigorous race? Some hoped for a victorious outcome, like Ginger, but others—*like Mr. Montrose, perhaps?*—would love a story of misfortune.

The qualifying athletes included three from Germany, two from Canada, and one each from America, Sweden, Japan, and Poland, along with the defiant Englishwoman, Nora Graves.

"Imagine running with all your might, non-stop for nearly half a mile?" Ginger said to Basil.

Basil shared her admiration.

The women runners lined up on the track. Nearly as many men, wearing white trousers, blue blazers, and flat-topped straw hats, stood on the sidelines officiating. Journalists pressed in like sniffing hounds.

The gun went off, and the women ran, arms pumping, legs with muscular definition working like pistons. The crowd was on its feet, people roaring, some with cries of exhortation, others with moans of displeasure. Ginger cheered as loudly as she could. *Why shouldn't these women be encouraged in sports? Go for it, ladies!*

The race ended with a victorious Lina Radke from Germany crossing the line for gold, with a historic silver medal win by Kinue Hitomi, the first Japanese woman ever to win an Olympic medal, and the bronze picked up by Sweden's Inga Gentzel.

The rest of the women staggered over the line. All were deeply winded, and some were in tears. Ginger couldn't help but seek out Nora Graves and her distinctive pigtails. She scanned the women until she saw Nora folded over at the waist and bracing herself with her hands on her knees.

A face from the past flashed before Ginger's eyes. She remembered now who Miss Graves reminded her of. A fellow spy from France. It'd been years, of course, and even then, Ginger's time with Edith Smythe had only been a few short weeks. It was so funny how the mind worked.

"I hope that stops all that nonsense talk that women can't be admirably athletic," Ginger said, feeling a flush of pride for her gender. A win for one woman was a win for them all.

Through her field glasses, she could see the activity on the track, the coaches encouraging their athletes and sometimes, consoling them. The officials were consulting together, making notes, and sending runners off with their final numbers. The journalists, including Mr. Bottomley's nemesis, Mr. Montrose, had scattered. Ginger caught sight of Mr. Bottomley's face before he disappeared, a look of disgruntlement etched in his features.

Ginger couldn't wait to read the reporting on this triumphant race.

She was to be sorely disappointed.

THE NEXT MORNING, Basil sipped coffee over a breakfast of fried eggs and a piece of spiced rye cake called *ontbijtkoek*, while enjoying a moment of quiet. Ginger had stepped out to collect the newspapers delivered to their hotel room door and hadn't returned. Basil could only assume the headlines had so captivated his wife, she hadn't left the corridor before reading them.

He hadn't anticipated the anger that accompanied Ginger's eventual return.

"Absolute rubbish!" She threw each paper with its front-page quote on the table one at a time. *"The Daily Mail*, with the headlines: *Women Athletes Collapse. Fierce Strain of Olympic Race–Sobbing Girls.* A front-page column in the *New York Evening Post: Below us on the cinder path were ten wretched women, five of whom dropped out before the finish, while five collapsed after reaching the tape."* Ginger was incredulous. "Was this reporter even there?"

And this from Mr. Bottomley. *"Young Nora Graves nearly sent to her grave.* Fancy taking a shot at a young woman who's already taking the brunt of public displeasure for going against the grain."

Basil wiped his lips with a cloth napkin, feeling a pang of disbelief. "Are you quite serious?"

"Serious as the sun currently beating on down the straw hats of these ridiculous men!" Ginger's wrath was something Basil rarely saw; however, it did nothing to diminish her beauty. How he landed such an extraordinary wife was something he'd never understand but would always be thankful for.

Ginger wouldn't be pleased if she knew how his thoughts had so easily strayed. He pulled his gaze from her blazing green eyes to the next paper she slammed onto the table.

"This is *Chicago*," she said tightly. *"Of the eight girls who finished, six fainted, exhausted—a pitiful spectacle and a reproach to anyone who had anything to do with putting on a race of this kind.* He couldn't even bother to get the numbers right. I'm furious, Basil. I could spit nails!"

Basil carefully pulled the remaining paper from Ginger's grip. "Sit down, love. Have a cup of tea."

Ginger breathed a sigh of resignation and slowly lowered herself into her chair. "Thank you, love," she said more calmly. "My having a fit won't solve the plight of women around the world who suffer injustice daily." She poured her teacup nearly full and added a spoon of sugar. "That last one by *The New York Times* is laughable."

Basil flicked the paper, making it taut, then read

aloud, "This byline is by a Jack Montrose. *'The gals dropped in swooning heaps as if riddled by machine-gun fire.'"* He whistled. "That's a blinder."

"This will set back women's athletics a dozen years," Ginger said wearily. "Mark my words."

"Let's not think about that over which we have no control," Basil said, reaching for her hand. "How would you like to spend the rest of the day?"

"If you'll recall, we're to join Felicia and Charles for luncheon," Ginger answered. "I don't feel like returning to the stadium, but I miss Scout. Shall we pop in to see him beforehand?"

"That's a splendid idea," Basil said. "Though I feel he's hardly missing us at all."

"Young boys, indeed young men, rarely consider their parents," Ginger said. She moved from the breakfast table to the bedroom and opened the wardrobe. She missed Lizzie giving her advice and assistance to get ready for the day. Buttons and snaps at the back were difficult, if not at times impossible. Thankfully she had Basil who helped her when needed, and with much enthusiasm.

Flipping through the day frocks hanging in front of her, Ginger selected a lovely yellow Lucile. More the colour of freshly churned butter than the starkness of a daffodil, it went well with her sun-kissed skin, and the soft-green embroidered print and matching ribbon, both at the neck and low on the waist, brought out the green in her eyes.

Summer days required less make-up, but never a day went by when one's eyebrows didn't require plucking. It took a bit of artistic flair to maintain the thin, high arch that was in fashion, not to mention a certain tolerance for pain. Ginger then applied a blue powder to her eyelids, brushed mascara onto her lashes, and added a spot of rouge to each of her cheekbones.

Pinning her red hair off her face, the bob straight rather than curly, she situated a lacy summer hat on her head. After snapping round pearl earrings on her earlobes, she lifted a necklace of a multi-strand of pearls which closed at the back of the neck with a small hook and eye. Ginger could easily manage it. She smiled wryly at her reflection in the mirror, then called over her shoulder. "Basil, love? Do you have a minute?"

CHAPTER SEVEN

The days fell into a pleasant routine, starting with Ginger and Basil sharing breakfast and reading the morning papers. Next, they checked the day's Olympic schedule and decided what events to attend. More than one competition happened at a time, not all at the stadium, so one had to choose judiciously. So far, they'd watched fencing, rowing, and cycling, but the highlight for Ginger had been the women's 100 metre relay race four days before. The Americans had taken silver after the triumphant Canadian team, with the German team coming in third. Ginger wondered how the British team would've fared had they competed.

"I'd like to go and watch the boxing today," Basil said as he casually sipped his tea.

Ginger wrinkled her nose. She'd had quite enough

of the "sport" of boxing. Scout's older cousin had got involved in underground fighting and had sustained a severe head injury. Ginger did her best to care for the young man, giving him work in the small stable behind Hartigan House.

"Don't forget, we have a luncheon at Charles and Felicia's place," Ginger said.

"Righto. Then we'll go and watch whatever is going on after that."

"I'm just happy they've found time for us," Ginger said, hoping she didn't sound put out. "Though, they've been rather elusive since we've been here, don't you think?"

Basil rubbed his smooth chin. "I suppose they have. They live here, so I imagine they have regular things to attend to. We have the privilege of being on holiday with heaps of time on our hands."

Ginger conceded, even so, an uneasiness gripped her. Was it disappointment she felt? She had hoped to spend more time with Felicia and had imagined them sitting in the stands together each day. Felicia always seemed to have an errand to run.

A knock on the door brought her out of her mood. Basil placed his napkin on his empty plate and pushed away from the table. "I'll get it."

Leaving Ginger to finish her breakfast, Basil strolled across the large room to the door, finding a sprightly youth about Scout's age, wearing a uniform with a navy-blue jacket with gold buttons and a jaunty-looking cap set at an angle on his head.

"Chief Inspector Reed," the lad said, his accent heavy.

"*Dat ben ik*," Basil returned, feeling trepidation.

In Dutch, the boy recited, "Message for you, sir. Inspector Van der Meer would like to speak to you. He's waiting in the lobby."

Basil pulled a coin from his trouser pocket and deposited it in the page's waiting hand. He returned in Dutch, "I'll be down shortly."

"What's that all about?" Ginger asked when he returned.

"Inspector Van der Meer from the police wants to speak to me."

Ginger's hand went to her throat. "It's not bad news from home, is it?"

"I doubt a page would've been sent to our room if that were the case. I'll head down to relieve our curiosity."

"Very well," Ginger said. "I'll go and see how Scout's doing, in the meantime."

BASIL MADE his way down to the lobby. As the bronze cage of the lift doors folded back, his gaze settled on a distinguished-looking man with a well-groomed moustache at the front desk. He wore a sharply tailored charcoal-coloured suit jacket over a crisp white shirt. A neatly knotted red cravat added an extra dash of formality. In his forties, he had dark hair touched with streaks of grey. And his blue eyes sparkled with keen intelligence. It was only when Basil's eyes briefly caught the glint of a polished badge pinned neatly to the lapel of the man's jacket that he realised this was a member of the –*Gemeentepolitie*—The Dutch Municipal Police.

"Ah, Chief Inspector Reed of Scotland Yard, I presume," the man said as Basil approached. His Dutch accent was heavy, but his English was clear and seemed to come easily.

Basil held out his hand. "Yes, I'm he."

"My name is Hoofdinspecteur Van der Meer from the police here in Amsterdam," the inspector returned as he heartily shook Basil's hand. "I find 'Inspector' acceptable if you prefer the English word."

"Nice to meet you," Basil said. "What can I do for you, Inspector?"

"First, my apologies for disturbing you. I know you are here on holiday."

"That's quite all right. I suspect you have good reason."

"Yes, a suspicious death occurred last night. The body is at the mortuary, waiting for the autopsy." Exhaling, he continued, "Chief Inspector Reed, we think the person is of British citizenship. Because of the Olympics, and the eyes of the world on us, so to speak, we made sure to contact Scotland Yard at once. They instructed us to seek you out here at Hotel Gouden Leeuw."

"I see. Did the Yard ask that I take part in the investigation?"

"Yes, as a consultant, if you would be willing. *I*, of course, am in charge of the investigation, but I would very much value your input on the matter as the case unfolds.

Basil stroked his chin. Hopes of a relaxing vacation would be dashed and Ginger wouldn't be pleased—unless he brought her on board as *his* consultant.

"As I said," Inspector Van der Meer continued, "newspapermen from around the world are gathered in our fine city, and it won't be long until the news gets out. This is an unfortunate matter. Having someone of your rank and influence within Scotland Yard on the case with us would make it clear that both the Dutch police and Scotland Yard are doing everything we can to get to the bottom of things."

"Where was the body found?"

"In the Wilgenbocht canal just on Lanenstraat, a small street in the south part of Amsterdam."

"So, the body was in the water?"

The inspector nodded gravely. "A canal fisherman discovered the body."

"What makes you think the death was suspicious rather than a mishap?

Inspector Van den Meer glanced about the lobby, which had become busier over the preceding few minutes.

"I would rather get into that down at the station, please."

"The thing is, I'm just on my way—"

"Basil?" Ginger came out of the lift.

Basil found her dazzling as usual, with her beautiful green eyes that glistened, a radiant smile, and gorgeous red hair that caught the eye. Basil never tired of seeing her; introducing her as his wife brought him endless delight. His lips pulled up as Ginger approached him and the inspector. "Inspector, this is my wife, Mrs. Reed. Ginger, this is Inspector Van der Meer of the police here in Amsterdam."

"Pleased to meet you, madam." Inspector Van der Meer's manner was polite, but he did not have a smile.

"The pleasure is mine, Inspector," Ginger said, her green eyes flickering with curiosity and a hint of impatience. She was clearly conscious of the ticking clock. "Basil, I've been informed by the front desk that a water taxi is scheduled to leave shortly."

"I'm afraid there is some urgency on the matter, Chief Inspector," Inspector Van der Meer said.

"Love, it seems the Dutch police need me."

Ginger's eyes flashed with disappointment for the briefest moment. "You must go then, naturally," she said. "I'll give your love to Scout."

"Of course," Basil said.

"Now, if you'll please accompany me." Inspector Van der Meer gestured to the main hotel doors, and Basil followed the man outside, his eyes lingering on the water taxi that motored down the canal and his wife waving to him.

CHAPTER EIGHT

Ginger travelled to the Olympic stables via a canal boat run by an enterprising boat owner. On a bright summer day like this one, the city seemed heavenly: verdant greens like cashmere wool, and the canals gleaming like giant diamond necklaces. It reminded her a little of Venice, with "streets" of water.

The stables were spacious and well ventilated, with specific grooming and veterinary care areas. Comfortable stalls contained premium straw bedding. Beyond the buildings were rings for warming up the horses and taking them through their paces. Each country had specific needs and regimes, both dietary and training. Populating the stables, along with the high-breed horses, were stable workers and grooms, of which Scout was one.

Ginger doubted Scout would be in the small room

he shared with another stable hand at this time of day and soon found him in one of the stalls, brushing down a beautiful chestnut-coloured Dutch warmblood. Scout murmured gently to the gelding as he carefully brushed its glossy black mane.

"Hello, Scout," Ginger said, not wanting to startle him.

"Mum!" Scout set the brush down, patted himself free of bits of straw, and stepped out of the stall towards Ginger. "Isn't this the best thing ever? I want to ride for Britain in the Olympics one day!"

"That's a grand endeavour," Ginger said with a smile.

Scout's gaze roamed behind her. "Where's Dad?"

"Oh, he's been asked to act as a consultant for the Dutch police over a matter concerning a British national. He'll come and see you later. Now, tell me about this lovely creature."

"This is Pegasus Pride. It's my responsibility to keep him groomed and warmed up. We're pretty good at jumping." He patted the flank of the horse's glossy neck, his cheek rosy with pride. "Ridden by Mr. Bernard Masters. Owned by Miss Marion Hughes."

Ginger wrinkled her brow. She had heard the owner's name before. Her father was an MP in Leicestershire. "Isn't Miss Hughes on the track team? Or is there another Marion Hughes?"

A female voice answered. "It's one and the same."

Ginger turned to the voice. "Oh, hello. I was just admiring your horse. He's very handsome."

Miss Hughes, a tall, formidable woman, entered the stall and nuzzled her horse's neck. "Isn't he just?" She eyed Ginger. "I'm at a disadvantage. You know me, but I'm in the dark about you."

"Where are my manners?" Scout said. He'd been eyeing Miss Hughes with a doe-eyed gaze of admiration. "Miss Hughes, this is my mother, Mrs. Reed. Mum, Miss Hughes, Olympian."

"How do you do," Ginger said, shaking the athlete's hand. "That's quite an accomplishment, to qualify in two completely different Olympic categories."

"I was brought up with horses, so this part was a matter of good luck, and really, it's Pegasus who qualified for his race. I don't ride him."

"How disappointing it must've been for you with the British women's track team boycotting the games."

"Yes." Miss Hughes' lips tightened. "It was frightfully disappointing. I would've liked to compete, but I am united with my team's decision."

"I take it you're unhappy with Miss Graves' decision to run."

"Of course," Miss Hughes said tersely. "Her defiance diminishes the sacrifice the rest of us are making." As if to control her emotions, she inhaled deeply and caressed Pegasus Pride before continuing. "But at least I can still compete through this fellow. My opportunity to run my race will return in the next summer

Olympics." She turned to Scout. "I can take over from here."

It was hardly a subtle dismissal. Never one to overstay her welcome if it was possible not to, Ginger said, "It was very nice to meet you, Miss Hughes. All the best to you, Pegasus Pride, and your rider. Scout and I will be cheering for all of you."

"Scout, *kom hier!*"

"That's Mr. Gerrit KIaassen," Scout said, breaking into a jog. "The veterinarian."

Ginger followed him down the passage along the row of stalls.

Mr. KIaassen was a sturdy-looking fellow with muscular arms under his shirt's rolled-up sleeves, a man clearly used to handling heavier patients. "Comfort the ol' boy, will ya lad," the man said with a mild Dutch accent. He dug through his medical kit with a look of confusion on his face. "I thought there were five."

"Five?" Scout asked.

The vet held a metal tubular contraption in the air. "Five syringes. I'm only counting four. Oh well, I'm sure it'll show up." He stroked the horse in question, whispering, "There, there. This will be quick. Just a bit of pain relief for the ol' boy." After administering whatever was in the syringe, he instructed Scout to take the gelding to its stall. Then, as if noticing Ginger for the first time, his eyes widened. "Oh, my apologies. I would have waited a moment if I knew a lady was present."

"I assure you, Mr. KIaassen, nothing offended my sensibilities. I served in the war."

"Ah, yes. The war made men of the ladies and women of the men."

"Oh mercy," Ginger said. "Surely not all men."

"I'm thinking of the wounded, madam. Both bodies and minds but forgive my callous statement. We're in peace now and displaying the strongest of the strong, whether it be beast or man . . . or woman."

"I take it you aren't a fan of the women's athletics."

"It's not for me to say, but I read the newspapers. The eight hundred metres was too much. It nearly crushed those women." He shook his head. "I don't understand why the gentler sex, who can now reclaim their femininity, would not do so."

"Perhaps they are tired of being told what to do," Ginger said, then softened her tone. "Everyone likes to feel like they have a choice."

"Exactly," Mr. KIaassen said as if she'd just agreed with him. "Choose to be a woman. Like you, my fair lady." He waved a hand up and down in her direction. "A lovely specimen. Now, how do I know you?"

"You don't, sir. I'm Scout's mother."

"*You're* Scout's mother?" The veterinarian barely contained his incredulousness.

"You seem surprised."

"Well, it's not my place, but the lad lacks a certain refinement."

The idea that she should educate the man by telling

him of Scout's journey from living on the streets to being adopted by her and Basil was fleeting. Instead, she said, "Just the way I like him."

"Mr. KIaassen, do you have a moment?"

Ginger turned to the male voice, distinctly British, and found a slight, stern-faced man standing behind her.

The veterinarian pushed up on his spectacles. "Mr. Masters. I'm in the middle of something."

"It's quite all right, Mr. KIaassen," Ginger said. "I was about to leave." She extended a hand to the jockey. "You must be Pegasus Pride's rider. I'm Mrs. Reed."

A hard-fought smile tugged at the man's lips. "I am, and it's a pleasure."

"I'm an acquaintance of Miss Hughes. And I understand my son, Scout, is helping you out."

For the first time, light entered the man's eyes. "Scout is your son, is he? He's a fine lad. And talented. I wouldn't be surprised to see him riding for Britain soon."

Ginger gushed. "That would be his dream come true."

When neither man spoke, Ginger excused herself, leaving them to their conversation. Mr. KIaassen's eyes clouded with displeasure, and Ginger wondered what about the rider triggered this response.

Her natural curiosity made her pause outside the office door, out of sight.

Mr. KIaassen's voice, loud with irritation, reached

her. "I told you, Masters, I'll get it. It's a busy time if you didn't notice."

One of the stable hands entered the corridor, and Ginger was forced to continue on her way. She'd yet to encounter any group that didn't engage in some drama, and those who gathered at the Olympic stables were no different.

CHAPTER NINE

Felicia had forgiven her husband.

Charles had always had a sense of mystery about him—it was what she'd found so alluring about him when they first met. He'd been confident and still carried himself with confidence and purpose, and as an earl, his presence captured the attention of both men and women. Men who wished they were as handsome, wealthy, and titled as Charles, and women who wanted to be his wife, or if that role was taken, his mistress.

Charles hadn't been unfaithful.

But he had lived a double life, and if Felicia's nature had been more docile, or if she'd been blessed with a quiver full of babies to distract her, she mightn't have noticed.

Or at least, she mightn't have been so miserable.

Felicia had been raised by a dowager, Lady

Ambrosia Gold, whose only goal, it seemed to Felicia, was to see her granddaughter married well. Anything from a baron and up would do, so when Charles Davenport-Witt, the Earl of Witt, took a fancy to Felicia, Grandmama was delighted.

As was Felicia. Her life had been so sheltered, she'd never known want—except to long for her parents, who had sadly died together on the same day, and for her only brother, Daniel, Ginger's first husband, who had passed away in the Great War. But physical needs, Felicia hadn't any. She had spent her youth antagonising her grandmother by engaging in the ways of flapper girls, not even trying to hide her disdain for the Victorian ways Grandmama embraced.

By the time Charles entered her life, Felicia was ready to step into a more mature role as wife and mother, leaving her party friends behind. Ambrosia had been filled with gratitude and relief.

And Felicia would be lying if the prospect of going from Miss Gold to Lady Davenport-Witt hadn't been a draw.

She should've been ecstatically happy.

The problem was that Charles *did* have another love interest: his country, which took the form of serving in the British secret service. The agency required so much of his time and attention that any lady would grow discouraged in her marriage, especially when she and Charles were still newlyweds. And when they lost the baby, and none other followed, Felicia felt utterly unanchored.

Until she realised that Charles worked as a secret agent for the British government. When she asked to join, he'd adamantly opposed her offer, but it was that or the end of their marriage.

Felicia feared he might choose the latter, but he conceded. He *did* love her and couldn't see going through life without her.

So, now they lived in a flat on the *Grachtengordel*, translated as The Canal Ring, a prestigious Amsterdam neighbourhood with man-made canals, rings within rings. Their cook was busy preparing the lunch that would be served when Ginger and Basil arrived.

Checking her wristwatch, Felicia wondered, *where is Charles?* He had had a man watching the target since early that morning. Charles was to check in with the man and then return.

After several weeks of training, which included surveillance and counter-surveillance, disguise and concealment, training Felicia had yet to use, cryptography, foreign languages, especially Dutch, some technical skills, and physical training, Felicia was thrilled to be given her first assignment in tandem with Charles. They were to locate a person of interest to the British government for reasons that hadn't been revealed to Felicia, and it was believed that their target might reach out to her younger sister, an athlete called Nora Graves, at the Games. It was Felicia and Charles' assignment to watch the sibling in hopes of spotting the elder sister. Charles had said as much, but he seemed to think this was a low-risk assignment that Felicia could handle.

Of course she could handle it! Weary, she knew it would require time to demonstrate her worth to Charles.

She had a knot in her stomach because they'd lost track of their target, and Felicia had a sinking feeling that something terrible had happened.

"Mevrouw?"

Felicia turned to the sound of her maid's voice. The girl immediately curtsied and asked if they should start putting out the food for lunch. In Dutch, Felicia told her they'd wait for the gentleman to arrive.

Finally, when the sound of the door locks unclicking—Charles insisted on several—could be heard, Felicia walked expectantly into the corridor and waited by the door.

"Charles?" she said as he stepped inside and dutifully re-engaged the locks.

As he shook his head, his dark hair, oiled heavily, remained unaffected. "Bouwens claims he took up his post at four this morning. When Miss Graves failed to come out of the guest house, he asked around, hoping the other athletes would know where she could be found, and no one knew. Finally, her roommate said she sneaked out last night and never returned."

Felicia's hand gripped the long strand of beads that

hung low over her chest. Losing sight of their target was terrible news, and Felicia couldn't help but take it personally. This was her first official case. She dreaded the thought of failing it. "What are we to do now?"

Charles rubbed the back of his neck. "Aren't Basil and Ginger on their way?"

"They should be here any minute."

"Then we eat lunch," Charles said. "Go on normally with our lives. Others are looking for her, and we can trust that they'll learn something of import shortly."

The bell rang, announcing someone at the door.

"Ginger and Basil," Felicia said knowingly. The maid released the locks and opened the door, but only Ginger was ushered into the drawing room.

"Where's Basil?" Felicia asked as she embraced Ginger in welcome.

"Strangely enough," Ginger said as she removed her gloves and set her purse on the side table, "the Dutch police required his assistance. Apparently, there's been a suspicious death involving a British national."

Felicia shared a quick look with Charles, who, with his years of training, didn't even show a flicker of alarm. Felicia didn't do as well at hiding her own.

"Oh dear," she said, leading Ginger into the sitting room.

The room, decorated in rich blues and purples, had many wooden tables and cabinets and, still reminiscent of the cluttered fashion of the Victorian and Edwardian eras, the walls were wallpapered and covered with framed paintings, a mix of Dutch landscapes and royalty. The blue settees and armchairs faced a brick fireplace.

"No one you know, I hope," Felicia continued, then added for clarity, "the dead British national."

"The identity is unknown; at least the police hadn't relayed it to Basil before he left with them." Ginger took in the flat, smiling with appreciation. "You have a lovely place here. What a tremendous view of the canal. You must love staring at it constantly."

While Ginger's back was turned, Charles nodded towards the door. He was leaving.

"Yes," Felicia returned, a moment later. "We can't get enough of it," she said. "It's convenient that Basil will be late, as Charles just remembered an errand he has to run. You don't mind if he goes, do you, Ginger?"

Ginger's green eyes flickered in Charles' direction, flashing briefly with suspicion, though Felicia couldn't think why.

"Of course not," Ginger said, taking a blue wing-backed chair. "You and I have much to discuss and catch up on while we wait. You must tell me all about your life in Amsterdam. I'm certain I'll be filled with envy."

Charles slipped away as Felicia took a seat next to Ginger. "By the time I've finished, you'll be begging Basil to move here too!"

Felicia instructed the maid to bring tea and a plate of cheese and biscuits to tide them over until the men returned and then turned to Ginger. She'd never thought she'd have to engage her training to have tea with her former sister-in-law, but it took all her might to act casual and interested and push all her questions about the body at the mortuary and the fact that they'd lost track of their target—

could they be one and the same?—out of her mind.

CHAPTER TEN

*D*r. Gregoor Jansen, the pathologist presiding over the Amsterdam mortuary, was a man whose appearance was as distinctive as his profession. Standing tall and lean, Dr. Jansen had neatly combed hair in a striking shade of silver, and his blue eyes, slightly enlarged through the lenses of his wire spectacles, conveyed a sense of keen awareness. Dressed in a pristine lab coat that accentuated his professional demeanour, he had an unmistakable precision, from his orderly attire to the methodical way he organised his workspace.

Like every mortuary Basil had ever visited, this one was starkly at odds with the bustling vibrancy of the city that surrounded it. The inside air was cool, still, and heavy with solemnity. The room for body examination was unadorned and functional. The steady glow of incandescent bulbs illuminated the pristine white walls. Along the walls were trays of scalpels, scissors, and forceps, all lying in a strictly ordered fashion. In the centre of the room stood a white ceramic examination table with a corpse lying on it.

"She was found by a canal fisherman early this morning," Inspector Van der Meer said.

Initially, Basil saw only the form of an apparent female drowning victim—pale and lifeless. But as he stepped closer, a realisation dawned on him. He recognised the woman. Her athletic physique, now motionless, and her facial features, although subdued in death's embrace, made her identity undeniable. The water from the canal had left its mark, her hair straggling—only one pigtail remained—damp clothing clinging to her form, a sombre testament to her final moments. It struck Basil as he regarded her lying on the cold table how stark the difference between her lifeless form was from the vibrant competitor he had recently seen at the Olympic stadium.

"This is Nora Graves," Basil said. "A British athlete."

Inspector Van der Meer nodded. "We welcome your confirmation.

"Determining the time of death may be challenging," Dr. Jansen said, "as cold water can affect the usual post-mortem changes in a body. I'll have to examine things like stomach contents, skin condition, and the state of rigor and livor mortis. But I think it's fairly safe to assume it happened early in the morning."

"The question is," Inspector Van der Meer started, "why was she out in the early morning hours?"

"Something, or more likely *someone*, drew her out," Basil said. "Or insomnia? She may have been restless and wanted space to roam."

Inspector Van der Meer raised a brow. "Was it an accident, then? Or foul play?"

"Or did she take her own life?" Basil offered. "Competition at this level is stressful, and the pressure on the women athletes has been particularly harsh."

The inspector postulated, "And Miss Graves buckled under it?"

Basil shrugged. "It's all speculation at this point. As far as I understand, the athletes had a curfew."

"Yes," the inspector said. "Over two hundred British athletes have been billeted in larger houses or school dormitories in areas of Amsterdam close to the Olympic venue."

BASIL WHISTLED. "Hopefully, someone on the Olympic organisational committee can tell us where Miss Graves was staying. There's a chance someone saw her leave."

"There is something else," Dr. Jansen said, taking a pencil from his lab coat pocket. "I just noticed this shortly before you gentlemen arrived, so I haven't yet had a chance to examine it thoroughly."

Dr. Jansen moved the right arm of the body to

expose the underarm. "I've observed a small puncture wound, approximately the size of a needle's point, located in a less conspicuous area of the body." He tapped the end of his pencil on the spot. "The surrounding tissue shows redness from slight inflammation. I will look for signs of trauma or natural disease. The puncture was made by something fine and sharp."

"A needle?" Basil asked.

"Possibly," the pathologist replied. "I will look for penetration depth, angle, and tissue reaction."

"What about the tissue reaction?" Basil asked.

Dropping the pencil into his pocket, Dr. Jansen said, "Some injections, if done improperly or with irritating substances, can cause tissue reactions, including inflammation, infection, or necrosis."

"What kind of irritating substances are possible?" Inspector Van der Meer asked.

"It could be many things. I can conduct tests of tissue, blood, or stomach contents." Dr. Jansen adjusted the spectacles on his nose. "As always, gentlemen, modern science can answer many of your investigative questions, but you have to allow for the due processes required for accuracy."

Basil caught the Dutch inspector's eye. "You have an intriguing case here, Inspector Van der Meer. How would you like to proceed?"

"I'll have my men track down the address where Miss Graves was staying and question the hosts. I'll send a message to your hotel when I have more information."

"Very well," Basil said, though he hated the thought of sitting around waiting. At least he had the luncheon with Charles and Felicia to help pass the time. And his stomach was grumbling. "I'll ring you this afternoon," Basil said. "And if I learn of anything of significance on my own, I'll be sure to inform you."

Inspector Van der Meer ducked his chin. "That would be appreciated, Chief Inspector."

CHAPTER ELEVEN

Ginger wondered if Basil and Charles would make it back before she and Felicia gave in to hunger, but as serendipity would have it, both men arrived simultaneously.

"Oh good," Felicia said with a note of relief. Turning to the maid, she said in Dutch, "Please advise Cook that we'll eat in thirty minutes."

"I'm impressed with your ease with the language," Basil said as he greeted Felicia. "Dutch isn't the easiest to learn."

"She's been a diligent student," Charles said with pride.

"Do you understand Dutch, Basil?" Felicia asked.

Basil nodded. "I have a rudimentary knowledge. My family often came here on holiday when I was a child."

Felicia led the way into the sitting room. The flat, taking up the whole floor, was exquisitely decorated and perfectly suited for an earl and countess. Ginger lowered herself onto the settee beside her husband, itching with curiosity about what the Dutch inspector had wanted him for. Alas, propriety called for restraint.

Basil crossed his legs languidly. "I still don't quite understand what propelled you to Amsterdam," he said. "Not that it isn't a most beguiling city."

The maid arrived with a tea tray, and Felicia poured and served. "We'll have a fresh pot with our meal."

"Felicia and I were discussing today's headlines," Ginger said.

Charles grinned. "I'm sure it has plenty of ladies in deep discussion."

"And men too, I hope," Felicia said, staring down her husband. "We women have finally been given the right to vote in the same manner as men, only to have something else taken away."

Ginger sighed. "It does feel like one step forward, two steps back at times."

"It's frightfully unfair," Felicia agreed.

"Indeed," Charles said. "But it hasn't been all bad news for the women athletes. Every woman's event has its gold medallist."

"As do the men's competitions, Charles," Felicia returned.

The maid announced that the lunch would soon be served, and Ginger followed Felicia into the dining room, which held a long, ornate table with matching chairs, over which hung an electric chandelier.

Once seated, they were served a simple meal which included soup, cold meat on pieces of heavy bread, salad, and a deep-fried roll-shaped item covered in breadcrumbs.

"This looks interesting," Ginger said, referring to the roll.

"It's call a *kroket*," Felicia said. "Or plural, *kroketten*. There's meat ragout inside."

Ginger found it delicious. The bread was wonderful as well, although heavier than commonly served in Britain. "Speaking of bread," she said, after she took a bite, "in a recent letter from my sister, Louisa, she wrote about bakers selling bread already sliced. A machine does it. A whole loaf sliced by many knives at once."

Basil laughed. "What will they think of next?"

"What is your favourite thing about Amsterdam?" Ginger asked as the meal began to wind down and tea was served again.

"I love all the water," Felicia said. "In London, one has to travel for hours to Brighton or Portsmouth to get to the sea."

"What about the Thames?" Basil said.

Felicia wrinkled her nose. "I suppose there's that, but I find it rather smelly."

Ginger set her gaze on Felicia's distinguished-looking husband. "What about you, Charles?"

"There is a lot of culture and history here, as there

is in Britain, but I've tired of those stories. It's nice to hear about something different.

"Such as?" Basil prompted.

"Have you heard about the Tulip Mania?" Felicia asked. "The demand for tulips in the 1630s drove the price for the bulbs unbelievably high. Some single bulbs sold for more than ten times the annual earnings of a skilled craftsman. It was madness, I tell you."

"Oh, that is interesting," Ginger said.

"Of course, the tulip market crashed dramatically," Charles added, "with many flower lovers none the richer. An economic cautionary tale if there ever was one."

"On another note of interest," Ginger said as she faced Basil. "Are you going to tell us about your excursion with the Dutch inspector?"

"I say, good fellow," Charles chimed in. "Is it true one of our own has met his demise?"

"Her demise, I'm afraid." Basil frowned. "I'm dreadfully sorry to have to announce that Miss Nora Graves was found deceased."

Felicia gasped sharply, her hand flying to her mouth a fraction too late to disguise it. Ginger raised a brow. "Did you know her?"

"No, of course not." Felicia cast her husband a quick sideways glance before continuing. "Just, I knew her by reputation. And we all saw her racing the eight hundred metres."

"Are you sure it's her?" Charles asked. "Not to be a

cad, but a lot of those young girls look the same if you ask me."

"I viewed the body myself," Basil said. "However, the police will probably track down next of kin or perhaps her roommate to confirm her identity."

"Did she have next of kin?" Felicia asked.

"Surely she must have someone," Ginger said. "A parent, or a sibling, or cousin."

"Quite," Felicia said. "It's just all so ghastly. A shadow cast over what is supposed to be a joyous gathering of nations."

Ginger thought Felicia was being a bit dramatic, but she wasn't wrong. It certainly was a tragedy.

"How did she die?" Charles asked.

"She was found in a nearby canal and presumed drowned," Basil said.

"But..." Ginger prompted.

"But the pathologist, Jansen, is a competent and experienced man. He found what he believes to be a pinprick under the arm."

"And that's caused you to be suspicious?" Charles asked. "Couldn't it be anything? An accident with a hat pin or brooch?"

"It could be," Basil said, "but I'm waiting for blood tests to rule out foul play. In the meantime, it's being investigated by the police as either an accident or perhaps suicide."

"Did anyone see her fall?" Ginger asked.

Basil shook his head. "No witnesses have come forward so far."

"A romantic assignation gone wrong?" Felicia offered.

"It wouldn't be the first time, my love," Charles said, taking her hand. "Not everyone is blessed with a love match such as we enjoy."

Ginger held back the smile that threatened. These two hadn't been enjoying the pleasures of a "love match" whilst living in London. "Amsterdam has certainly done you two the world of good," she said.

"Indeed," Charles agreed, then glanced pointedly at his wristwatch.

"Is there somewhere you need to be?" Ginger asked.

"It would be rude of us," Charles said, "but I've accidentally committed myself and my wife to be somewhere else this afternoon as well."

"You two go along," Ginger said. This unconventional change of plans by their hosts suited her. She was eager to get Basil alone and sensed there was more to Nora Graves' death story than he was letting on.

"Are you sure you don't mind?" Felicia said.

"Not at all." Ginger grabbed Basil's arm. "We have things to take care of as well, haven't we love?"

"We have," Basil responded jovially.

Goodbyes were said and promises made to meet up again shortly. Once Ginger and Basil were alone outside, Ginger cocked her head and said, "Shall we visit Miss Graves' hostess?"

CHAPTER TWELVE

*A*msterdam bustled with energy, not only because the city was hosting the Games but also because other cultural exhibitions, including many museums and historic sites, brought people out in droves. Ginger enjoyed being part of it and admired the architecture—many tall, narrow houses with gabled façades—along with the picturesque parks and glistening canal systems. The taxicab stopped in front of one of the tall houses.

"How do you know where Miss Graves was staying?" Ginger asked before stepping out of the vehicle.

"The good folks at the police station provided me with the address," Basil said. "They had the foresight to contact the Olympic committee and ask for a list of all the visiting athletes." Checking his notes again, he pointed. "It's that one."

The door was answered by a weary-looking woman

dressed in a day frock and flat leather shoes, her salt and pepper hair pulled back into a bun. She muttered something in Dutch.

"I'm sorry," Basil said. "Do you speak English?"

"I am full," she returned in heavily accented English.

"We're not looking for a room," Ginger said. "We'd like to ask a few questions about Miss Graves."

"Juffrouw Graves not here."

"Have the police been here already?" Basil asked.

"*Ja*. Very sad."

"I'm Chief Inspector Reed of Scotland Yard and this is my wife, Mrs. Reed," Basil said. "We are working with the Dutch police, investigating Miss Graves' death. You must be Mevrouw Beekhof."

"Ja, ja." Opening the door, the woman stepped out of the way and motioned for them to come inside. "I talk to police this morning. Nothing new."

"We only want to confirm the details," Basil said, removing his hat. "It won't take long."

They were directed to sit in the living room. Two blue velvet settees faced each other in front of a red-brick fireplace. An ornate wooden coffee table sat between them.

"They ask me to take in two girls from England," Mrs. Beekhof said, sitting on a settee as Ginger and Basil sat on the one opposite. "I know a bit of English, so."

"Besides Miss Graves, who else is staying here?" Ginger asked.

"Juffrouw Hughes."

"The equestrian?" Ginger said with a note of surprise. "Horses?" she added at Mrs. Beekhof's confused look.

"Ja, horse. Nice girl. Not here. Gone to stables."

"I met her when I visited Scout," Ginger said to Basil. "She owns one of the horses competing in the Games."

Basil raised a dark brow. "Interesting coincidence." To Mrs. Beekhof, he asked, "What was Miss Graves like? Was she a good guest?"

Mrs. Beekhof offered another shrug. "Quiet. Not so very friendly. But no trouble until now. Juffrouw Hughes tells me Juffrouw Graves left in the middle of the night." With a deep frown of disapproval she added, "This is not allowed."

Ginger heard the front door open and turned to see Miss Hughes come through the sitting-room door. Mrs. Beekhof got to her feet. "Juffrouw Hughes. Come, please." The hostess seemed pleased to have someone to share her company with. "English couple here to ask about Juffrouw Graves."

Miss Hughes wore her jodhpurs, a short jacket, and riding boots. Her eyes widened with recognition when her gaze landed on Ginger. "Scout's mother?"

"Hello again," Ginger said. "I'm also the wife of Chief Inspector Reed from Scotland Yard."

Basil stood to shake Miss Hughes' hand. "Because

Miss Graves is a British national, I've been asked to assist."

"Assist? Has she been kidnapped?"

Mrs. Beekhof jumped in. "She was not here when the police came."

"What's happened?" Miss Hughes asked. "Is Nora in trouble?"

"I'm afraid the news is bad," Basil said. "Her body was found this morning."

Miss Hughes blanched. She reached for the nearest chair and lowered herself into it.

"We've been told that Miss Graves left this house in the early hours," Basil said. "Would you know what time?"

"I heard her leave our room at two. I know because I had to use the bathroom and waited for her to return. I wondered what was taking her so long, so after fifteen minutes, I investigated, concerned there might be a problem. But she wasn't there."

"Do you know why she might have left like that?" Ginger asked. "Had she complained about having trouble sleeping?"

Miss Hughes shook her head. "No, she slept like a log. I envied her that. If anything, I have trouble sleeping, but it never occurred to me to break curfew to go for a walk in the middle of the night."

Ginger didn't miss the judgemental note in Miss Hughes' statement. "Why do you think she left? To meet someone, perhaps?"

Miss Hughes hesitated. "It's not really my place to talk."

Basil cleared his throat. "Might I remind you that a death has occurred."

"Is it suspicious? It must be, mustn't it? I mean, otherwise, why would you be here? You think Nora was murdered. Was she? Was she murdered?"

Mrs. Beekhof emitted a strangled sound before falling back into her chair.

"We can't deny or confirm that at this time," Basil said. "We are merely doing our due diligence in the hope of finding the truth."

Miss Hughes placed her fingertips on her forehead as if propping her head up. "She might've been meeting Mr. Dankworth."

"Claude Dankworth?" Ginger asked. "The coach of the British women's athletic team?"

"Yes. Though I don't know why he's even here, with the team boycotting the event." Miss Hughes sniffed. "Except that Nora came."

"Are you implying that Mr. Dankworth and Miss Graves were involved romantically?" Basil asked.

Miss Hughes huffed. "Are you surprised because Mr. Dankworth is married? Or because he's the coach?"

"Both reasons are regrettable," Ginger said. "So, were they?"

"Yes," Miss Hughes said simply. "We all warned Nora to stay away from him, but . . ."

"But?" Ginger prompted.

"Nora seemed to imply that she tried. I think Mr. Dankworth was a little obsessed with her."

"Mrs. Beekhof," Basil said, "would you mind if my wife and I took a look at Miss Graves' room?"

Ginger knew the woman would be more likely to let Basil in if she was with him, and she was correct in that assumption.

Mrs. Beekhof shrugged again, a habit, Ginger realised by now. "If you like. It is Juffrouw Hughes' room too."

Miss Hughes got to her feet. "I'll show you the way."

The wooden steps were steep and narrow, and their combined footsteps filled the passageway. Miss Hughes stopped on the landing of the third floor. "We get a workout every day." She opened the door to one of the rooms and then stepped aside. "Nora's bed is the one closest to the window."

The bedroom was tidy, with two single beds draped with colourful hand-quilted blankets along one wall and two matching desks along the opposite wall. Long curtains flanked the single window that looked out onto the street below.

Basil opened the drawer in Nora's bedside table. "A Bible, lip ointment." He lifted a book into the air. "*Ashenden: or The British Agent.*" He raised a brow. "Interesting choice."

Ginger glanced away. "The Great War is still of great interest to many people." She'd found the novel by W. Somerset Maugham intriguing and wondered if perhaps she should put pen to paper about the female secret agents who risked life and limb during the war—using a nom de plume, of course.

Ginger searched the desk but found nothing unusual—stationery and writing implements. But her eye caught the small rubbish bin between the desk and the wall. She plucked a crumpled piece of paper from it and smoothed it out. "Basil, look."

Basil read over Ginger's shoulder.

Nora, please meet me at the Wilgenbocht Canal at midnight. We need to talk.

"It's unsigned," Ginger said, "but Miss Graves must've recognised the handwriting. I doubt she would've gone if she didn't know the owner of this missive."

"Unless someone forged it," Basil said. "It is a rather short note."

"Very true, love," Ginger said. "At least we know Miss Graves left to meet someone and wasn't just wandering about with a case of insomnia. Let's show it to Miss Hughes. Perhaps she'll recognise the writing."

Miss Hughes was conveniently found hovering at the doorway. "Have you quite finished?" she asked with a tone of annoyance.

Ginger empathised. No one enjoyed the prospect of the police sniffing about their bedroom.

"Thank you for your understanding, Miss Hughes,"

Basil said. He held out the note. "We found this balled up in the rubbish bin."

Miss Hughes' expression hardened as she read it.

"Do you know who wrote this?" Ginger asked. "Do you recognise the handwriting?"

"It might be from Mr. Dankworth," Miss Hughes said stiffly.

"The British coach?" Basil clarified.

"Yes. Now, if you'll excuse me." Miss Hughes nodded towards the door, suggesting that Ginger and Basil had overstayed their welcome.

As they headed down the staircase, Ginger glanced back at the open bedroom door, catching Miss Hughes' narrow disapproving glare before she disappeared into her bedroom, slamming the door behind her.

CHAPTER THIRTEEN

Claude Dankworth proved difficult to track down. Ginger and Basil arrived at the Olympic stadium just as the gymnastics competitions began. The stadium buzzed with excitement as the women gymnasts gathered, the first time for women in Olympic history, though they could only compete in the all-around category. A deafening, home-crowd cheer rose as the Dutch team came on to the field.

"There's Mr. Bottomley," Ginger said, pointing to where the British journalist stood with his literary peers. "Perhaps he knows where we can find Mr. Dankworth."

"Mr. Bottomley!" Ginger called loudly. "Hello."

The small man turned, his frown a flicker before pulling into an insincere smile. "Mrs. Reed, Chief Inspector Reed. This is unexpected."

"Indeed," Basil said. "We're hoping you can help us."

Mr. Bottomley waved to the event unfolding on the field. "I'm rather busy, as you can see."

"This will only take a minute," Basil pressed. "We're looking for Mr. Claude Dankworth."

Mr. Bottomley's brows furrowed. "Who?"

"The coach for the British women's athletic team," Ginger said. "You must've interviewed the man for your paper."

"Oh, yes, of course," Mr. Bottomley sputtered. "Why do you want him?"

"We have a few questions," Basil said. "Do you know where the man is?"

"I haven't seen him since yesterday." Mr. Bottomley wrinkled his short nose. "He's a bit of a miserable so-and-so, if you know what I mean."

"Would you happen to know where he's staying?" Ginger asked. "Did he reveal that information to you?"

Mr. Bottomley flipped through his ever-present notebook, each page making a *whisp* sound until his stubby finger poked at an entry. "I talked to him after the eight hundred. He wasn't too pleased, I'll tell you. Hum, didn't get to anything personal like where he's staying."

Ginger exhaled her disappointment. It had been a long shot, anyway. "Thank you, sir."

"The Olympic organizers might know," Mr. Bottomley added helpfully and directed them to the information desk. "Now, if you don't mind." He nodded to the field again. "I do believe the Dutch team is going to take the gold."

Ginger and Basil had to manoeuvre through the thick crowds from the stadium to a room near the entrance where administrative matters were taken care of. A clerk stared at them suspiciously over gold-rimmed spectacles. "We're not supposed to give out personal information about our athletes or their coaches."

Basil reached into his jacket pocket and produced his police identification card. "I'm Chief Inspector Basil Reed of Scotland Yard and am working in connection with the Gemeentepolitie. This is police business. It's imperative that I locate Mr. Dankworth immediately."

"Oh, in that case . . ." The clerk pushed up on his glasses and removed a large binder from the shelves behind him. Opening it, he quickly found the tab he was looking for and opened the folder, flipping pages with a thin finger until he found what he was looking for. "According to our records, Mr. Dankworth was staying at a guesthouse. But he's returning to England today."

"How do you know?" Ginger asked.

"He happened to drop in this morning, as he had a key to return. I spoke to him myself."

They thanked the clerk and hurried outside, Basil waving down the nearest taxicab. "To the nearest motorcar hiring company, my good man," he instructed the driver.

"Mr. Dankworth is obviously desirous to leave the country," Ginger said. "But one would think he would've tried to leave this morning rather than this afternoon."

"Perhaps he had too much to drink and didn't awake until noon."

"It's possible. Especially if he drank because he . . ." She glanced at the listening driver, and even though she knew he likely could not understand, she lowered her voice. "Because of what happened. Whether it was an accident or intentional."

They arrived at the car hire company and rushed inside, Ginger on Basil's heels, Basil with his hand on his hat, only to stop short when the clerk immediately started shaking his head. *"Alle auto's zijn verhuurd."*

Basil frowned. "All the motorcars have been hired out."

Just as he spoke, a motorcar puttered to a stop outside the shop window. Basil pointed and said something in Dutch.

The man nodded. "Ja."

After signatures on paperwork and the cash exchange, the clerk handed over the keys, which had been so recently returned to him. Ginger snatched them up before Basil could drop his wallet back in his jacket pocket.

"Ginger?"

"They drive on the right side of the road," Ginger

said as she hurried to the door. "I learned to drive in America, so I'm more qualified."

Ginger had to concede that it took a bit to reacquaint herself with driving a machine set to motor along the right and noticed Basil grimacing as the gears ground.

"Don't worry, love," she shouted over the engine noise. "Just a little rusty!"

The drive to the ferry was rather long, taking a good couple of hours, but pleasant enough. Large portions were pastures and fields, dotted occasionally with small towns, the outskirts of The Hague being the exception. Ginger felt they were making good time as she kept the accelerator to the floor as much as possible. She couldn't help that the road itself wasn't always up to task.

"Blimey!" Basil shouted with exuberance when Ginger suddenly had to slam on the brakes to allow for the passing of a flock of sheep.

"Where's the fire?" he said when Ginger passed a slow-moving motorcar, waving to the stunned-looking driver and his equally baffled-looking passenger.

"We've got to get there before Mr. Dankworth catches the ferry," Ginger shouted. She noticed he held on to his hat when she manoeuvred around a sharp bend and grinned at his silliness—as if he could lose his hat whilst sitting inside a motorcar with the roof up.

Ginger was surprised at the number of people heading west to England via the ferry service, considering the Olympic Games were still well underway. It proved that not everyone was caught up in the excitement and that life went on as usual for many people.

Pulling sharply to a stop, Ginger stared at Basil with wide eyes. "Wasn't that fun?"

Basil straightened his collar. "Tremendously. But perhaps you'll give me a chance for similar enjoyment on the trip back?"

"I suppose that's only fair," Ginger conceded. Locking up the hired motorcar, they entered the ferry terminal.

Having never spoken to the coach in person, Ginger didn't immediately know which of the many men, dressed similarly in summer suits and hats, was the coach. She mentally weeded out the ones not travelling alone until she found a solitary figure she recognised from a newspaper picture she'd seen. His shoulders slumped, the man stared despondently at his feet,

"This way," Ginger said, tugging on Basil's arm.

"Mr. Claude Dankworth?"

The man startled, his eyes answering Ginger's voice, confirming that he was Mr. Dankworth. In a wasted effort, he attempted to smooth out his wrinkled suit jacket and straighten his tie. "Yes. And you are?"

Basil stepped in and introduced them. "I'm afraid I can't let you get on that ferry, Mr. Dankworth," he said.

The man gaped, his eyes flashing with offence. "Why on earth not?"

"Were you in the company of Miss Nora Graves last night?" Ginger asked.

"As it turns out," Mr. Dankworth said with a huff, "I was not."

Basil pulled out the letter they'd found in Miss Graves' rubbish bin. Ginger had smoothed it out, but the wrinkles were clearly imprinted. "We found this letter written by you that would suggest otherwise."

"She threw it in the bin?" Mr. Dankworth said incredulously.

"Did you meet her, Mr. Dankworth?" Basil pressed.

"I went to the Wilgenbocht canal by the triple lamppost, but she wasn't there. Granted, I was a bit late, damn drink, but she could've waited a few minutes, couldn't she? We were going through a rough patch, and I was hoping for a reconciliation. A midnight rendezvous—with all the strict chaperoning rules—was the only way I could see her alone. But hey, what's this all about? Why do you care?"

"Miss Graves's body was discovered this morning," Basil said.

Ginger watched the coach's reaction. He froze then let out a hoarse laugh. "No, that's not true. And it isn't funny, Chief Inspector."

Ginger didn't know if the man was sincere or disillusioned. He was in shock or a good actor. "Mr. Dankworth, I have to confirm that what the chief inspector is saying is true."

Basil took the man's arm. "Please come with us to

the police station, sir. We have a few questions to ask before you will be permitted to leave the country."

"But wait, this is a ghastly mistake. I didn't kill anyone."

"No one is accusing you of such a thing, Mr. Dankworth," Basil intoned as he guided the man through the crowds. "But I'm sure you are anxious to help the police solve the mystery behind the death of one of your athletes."

CHAPTER FOURTEEN

When Basil indicated that Ginger probably wouldn't be welcomed into the interview room with the Amsterdam police (as she sometimes was in London), she took a separate taxi back to the Olympic stadium. Whatever claims Mr. Dankworth made would need to be supported by others, and who better to talk to than Miss Graves' fellow track athletes?

Unfortunately, many athletes had returned to their home countries after their events were over, with the exception of the Americans. The entire American team had travelled over the Atlantic to the Netherlands on the SS *President Roosevelt*, a dedicated steamship that, once docked, served as the team's floating hotel.

The gymnastic events had been completed. Mr. Bottomley had guessed correctly, and the Dutch women's team had won gold. Next, the field was set up for the start of the equestrian competitions.

One by one, the horses and riders performed a series of predetermined graceful movements called dressage. Ginger thought of it as a ballet in the equestrian world. Mr. Masters and Pegasus Pride were announced. Ginger found she was holding her breath as she watched the duo. Most of what Ginger knew about this sport she'd learned from Scout. She brought her son into view through her field glasses and laughed as she watched him jump and pump his fist into the air.

Bernard Masters handed the reins to Scout, who, leading Pegasus Pride, disappeared through one of the exits.

Miss Hughes approached Mr. Masters, and instead of the congratulatory cheer that Ginger had expected to be shared between them, they stopped two feet from each other and stared as competitors might. Perhaps it wasn't so unusual as Miss Hughes came from an elite family, and Mr. Masters was in her employ, though Ginger thought a good performance at the Olympics should make room for some light-heartedness.

Not only did they not smile at each other, but Miss Hughes was almost scowling. Mr. Masters said something; Ginger couldn't see his lips enough even to guess, but whatever it was, Miss Hughes responded by pivoting on her heel and storming away.

Mr. Masters might be a great rider but was terrible at his social game.

The American athletes not competing sat in a group in a reserved section. Ginger made her way to the stands, cupping a hand over her eyes to reduce the glare as she searched for a familiar face. Eventually, she came across one. Miss Charlotte Hartley was one of the athletes who had competed in the women's athletics alongside Nora Graves. Perhaps she would offer insight into the situation.

Wearing a billowing summer frock with a large floral print, T-strap shoes, and her hair garnished with an oversized fabric daisy, Ginger garnered the attention of both the male and female spectators in the group. Though she didn't do it on purpose, she'd been told by those close to her, Felicia and Haley Higgins, to be precise, that she had a way about her that made people acquiesce. That translated into men standing to give her room as she walked by, tipping their hats in respect, and women shifting their knees to the side, their glances flashing anything from disinterest to envy to delight, depending on how they viewed Ginger, friend or foe, or neither.

Miss Hartley stared with disinterest as Ginger approached, prepared to move her knees out of the way. She had a boyish appearance, her hair shaved rather close to her neck, and she wore a bland, shapeless day frock. Her eyes rounded with surprise when Ginger claimed an empty seat beside her instead of passing by.

"Miss Hartley, right?" Ginger said, using her American accent, something she did rarely. Having spent much of her youth in Boston, the twang naturally returned to her. "I hope you don't mind if I take this seat."

"Not at all," Miss Hartley said, then focused on the dressage event happening on the field.

"Such control by both man and beast," Ginger said casually. "It must feel fabulous to have such control of your body like that. I've got two left feet, but you ran the eight hundred metres, didn't you?"

"You saw that, huh," Miss Hartley said with a note of bitterness. "Did you read what they said about us? Such hogwash! I could kill that Jack Montrose with my own hands."

"Yes, I read the *Chicago* coverage." Ginger played the devil's advocate. "You don't think he had a point, though? It looked like a tough race to me. And that wasn't the only scandal. Did you know the British team boycotted the event?"

"Of course I knew that. The Brits are soft, that's what."

"Well, not all, surely. What about that Nora Graves girl? She did all right."

"She came in sixth," Miss Hartley said. "Hardly worth the coverage she got. She'd have gone unnoticed if it weren't for her lazy teammates."

"Like you went unnoticed?" Ginger said softly. Miss Hartley gave her a heated look. "No offence, dear," Ginger added, lightly. "There are thousands of athletes.

Not all of them can get their names in the papers." She lowered her voice conspiratorially. "But you know what I heard, not to gossip, but it is quite salacious."

Miss Hartley couldn't resist. "What did you hear?"

Ginger pulled on the strong hint given by Miss Hughes. "Miss Graves was in cahoots with her coach. In a romantic way, if you get my meaning."

"Was she now," Miss Hartley returned dryly.

"You didn't know? I thought, being close like you athletes are . . ."

"We're not close, ma'am. We're *competitors*."

"I get the feeling you don't like the British."

"So? No law saying I have to."

"Ah, yes. Well, I've also heard something rather tragic."

Miss Hartley rolled her eyes.

"Apparently, Miss Graves has come to a dire end."

"What do you mean?"

"She fell into the canal."

Turning her head sharply, Miss Hartley asked, "How do you know this?"

"Ladies like me have connections, dear. What's more, the police are calling it suspicious. You wouldn't know who might've wanted Miss Graves out of the way. One of her *competitors*, maybe? I understand things can get quite heated with everyone wanting the gold medal. I saw you push Miss Graves, you know."

Miss Hartley's face blanched before flushing red. "What are you talking about?"

"Before the one hundred metres. You bumped into her at the start of the race.

"I was only trying to unsettle her. I'd never do anything to actually hurt her. Or anyone."

"Of course not, dear." Ginger shifted to face Miss Hartley. "Can you think of anyone who *would* hurt her?"

"I don't know. Why do you care?"

"Like I said, I have connections. And those connections will be interested in hearing about anyone who might've had something against Miss Graves. You came in seventh, didn't you?"

"You're barking up the wrong tree, ma'am."

"What tree should I be 'barking up'?"

"I've heard that Marion Hughes has a thing for Dankworth."

"Really?" Ginger couldn't see the appeal, but there was no accounting for taste. Perhaps that was why she was so cold when Mr. Dankworth's letter to Nora Graves had been produced. "Isn't he a married man?"

Miss Hartley huffed. "Some people don't care about that sort of thing, not if they can get something else out of it."

"Like a gold medal?" Ginger asked.

"Exactly."

"But Miss Hughes didn't compete in the athletics this year."

"She boycotted the events to stay on Mr. Dankworth's good side."

"He didn't like the boycott?" Ginger said, surprised. "He seemed to support Nora Graves, who didn't boycott the races."

"His support of Nora Graves had nothing to do with his feelings about the boycott. He was smitten with her."

"I thought you said you didn't know anything about them?"

Miss Hartley smirked but said nothing in reply.

"How do you know Miss Hughes' reasons for boycotting the events?" Ginger asked, trying again.

Miss Hartley scoffed. "She told me herself. In her mind, this is a temporary setback. She believes, with Mr. Dankworth's attention, she'll win a gold at the next Olympics."

"A forward thinker, is she?" Ginger said. Having obtained the information she was after, she got to her feet. "Thank you for the chat, Miss Hartley. It was enlightening."

Ginger made her way towards the entrance, wondering if the information office had a telephone. She could ring Basil at the police station to tell him about Miss Hughes and her involvement with Mr. Dankworth. Her mind was so focused on this next task and the ramifications of what this liaison could mean that she almost missed seeing Mr. Bottomley on the opposite side of the entrance.

The journalist was conversing with a lady whose face was obscured by the positioning of Mr. Bottomley's body, but by how he flung his short arms, it was clear they were having a row. Then, Mr. Bottomley shifted to the side, and his companion was revealed.

Ginger gasped. The woman in question was none other than Felicia! What on earth did she have to do with the British journalist, and what could she be rowing with him about?

Something stopped Ginger from interfering. The heated discussion was short-lived; Felicia and Mr. Bottomley split up and left in opposite directions. Ginger impulsively stepped in beside two strapping male athletes shielding her from view. She didn't want Mr. Bottomley to know she had seen the two of them. When he stormed off, Ginger pivoted back and ran after Felicia.

CHAPTER FIFTEEN

The interview room at the *Politiebureau* Amsterdam—the Amsterdam Main Police Station—bore the unadorned, windowless simplicity that befitted any room meant for such solemn purposes. A solid wooden table, flanked by chairs that had no doubt known countless occupants, was at its centre. The walls were bare save for a few faded maps and official edicts such as legal updates or internal guideline reminders. A solitary bulb dangled overhead, casting more shadows than light across the conversation.

Inspector Van der Meer sat directly across from Claude Dankworth, who sat smoking a cigarette; his hand trembled as he lifted it to his lips. Basil sat on Van der Meer's left and observed Dankworth's responses.

"Yes, we were seeing each other romantically," the British coach admitted. "It was supposed to be a discreet relationship, but I think that ship sailed a while ago."

"What do you mean?" Van der Meer asked. "Are you saying your relationship was known amongst the other athletes?"

"Probably, although no one ever mentioned it to me." Dankworth nodded. "But I think we've been seen together enough in England, even away from the athletic club facilities I trained them in. It's enjoyable gossip fodder."

Basil's eyebrows furrowed. "It's my understanding that you have a wife."

"On paper, yes," Dankworth said through a puff of smoke. "That's another ship that has sailed. Frances and I haven't had a real marriage for a long time. We've slept in different rooms for over five years. It's not a secret. Actually, we started formal plans for a divorce just before I came here. As we speak, she's probably at the solicitor's office in London."

"So, she didn't come to Amsterdam, then?" Van der Meer asked.

Dankworth shook his head sharply. "No, she's never had any interest in athletics, not even in the spirit of national pride that the Olympic Games rouse in most people."

Basil shared a quick look with Van der Meer. In the case of a murdered lover, the jealous spouse was usually the first suspect. They would need to confirm the whereabouts of Mrs. Frances Dankworth. Basil would ring Scotland Yard himself right after this interview.

"In case you were wondering . . ." Dankworth tapped a long piece of ash into the tray given to him. "Frances knows about Nora and me. I admitted it to her about six months ago. She was terribly upset at first, you know, but it was one of the things that propelled her to agree to a divorce, eventually."

"All the same," Basil said, "we'll have to contact her."

Dankworth nodded despondently. "Has she really gone?" Until now, the man had acted rather stoically about everything, but his eyes had welled up. "I mean, you definitely confirmed it was her body?"

"I'm afraid so," Van der Meer said.

"And you say she drowned in the canal?"

"Cause of death hasn't been determined," Basil said. "We're waiting for the pathologist's report."

"Dear lord." Dankworth rapidly blinked as he stared at his hand holding the cigarette. "I can't believe it."

"Mr. Dankworth," Basil began, "do you know if Miss Graves could swim?"

Dankworth slowly shook his head. "Honestly, the topic never came up."

"How long have you been seeing her romantically?" Inspector Van der Meer asked.

Dankworth rubbed a teary eye with a palm. "It started eight, nine months ago."

"Where were you just before you left to see her?"

Basil asked. "You mentioned something about drinking?"

"I was in my quarters."

"Alone?" Inspector Van der Meer raised a brow.

"I'm afraid so," Dankworth said weakly. "Someone gave me a bottle of that genever, or whatever it's called."

"Oude jenever?" Inspector Van der Meer said. "A favourite in Holland."

"Yes, that's it. Like a good London Dry Gin, only even better. Anyway, I had too much of it and fell asleep."

"Did anyone see you leave when you finally went to meet her?" Van der Meer asked.

"Not that I know of, but it's possible."

Basil scratched his temple. "Why were you trying to leave Holland today?"

"Well, I can see now why you would think that suspicious." Dankworth blew air out of his cheeks. "The truth is, now that the women's athletic events are over, I have no real interest in being here anymore. And when Nora, Miss Graves, didn't . . . when I thought she'd snubbed me last night, I decided to go back to London." Huffing long and hard, he added, "The Olympics have disappointed me greatly."

"What do you know about Miss Marion Hughes?" Basil asked.

Dankworth gaped in surprise at the sudden change of topic. "Well," he said after an extended pause. "She's a brilliant athlete, actually. I had hopes for a gold medal with her. She chose to boycott the races but came to the Olympics anyway. Because of her horse. Her family is well off."

Basil looked at him evenly. "I sense there's more you can tell me."

The British coach sucked air in through his teeth as he stubbed out his cigarette butt. "Miss Hughes likes to be the centre of attention. I gather she was spoilt as a child. Liked to spend more time with me than was necessary, as far as I was concerned, anyway."

Inspector Van der Meer looked up from his notes. "Can you expand on that?"

"She doesn't like to share the spotlight in any way, even when it comes to training. As soon as my attention moves to another, she becomes moody and petulant. She often tries to monopolise my time, interrupting others to redirect the focus to herself. Once, I swear she feigned an injury, a sprained ankle, just so she could be alone with me. It was truly miraculous how well her ankle had healed by the next day, no bruising or swelling. Several times, I've caught her rolling her eyes or making snide remarks under her breath when I've praised another athlete's progress."

"Like Nora Graves?" Basil asked.

"Especially her. Once, Miss Hughes showed up at a restaurant where Nora and I were dining and got a table within earshot. It was frightfully uncomfortable." He shuddered at the memory. "If it wasn't for the fact that her family is a generous supporter of the team, I would've cut her from it long ago."

Inspector Van der Meer tapped his pencil on his notepad. "Do you think Miss Hughes would go so far as to harm Mis Graves physically?"

Dankworth took his time answering. "I can't imagine that she'd actually kill her, if that's what you mean."

Basil thought of a phrase from a poetry book he had once read. As a detective, he'd often pondered the wisdom of the sentiment: In the turbulent soul, the seeds of violence are hidden, only awaiting the right storm to bloom.

CHAPTER SIXTEEN

Felicia was stunned to hear Ginger's voice calling her, and so soon after her encounter with Bottomley!

"Ginger," she said, panting slightly, vexed at the heat she felt spreading across her cheeks. "You didn't say you were coming back to the stadium."

"Neither did you."

Ginger's eyes were soft, but Felicia noted a stiffness in her delivery, which made Felicia believe she'd been caught out. Ginger's next words proved it. "It appeared like you were in the middle of a row with Mr. Bottomley. Do you know the journalist?"

"I do now," Felicia said. The aggravation she hoped to portray was very real indeed. "The oaf bumped into me and stamped on my foot without a word of apology. He made it sound like I was the one who'd run into him!"

Ginger patted Felicia's arm in solidarity. "My experience with the man confirms his lack of manners and grace. You mustn't let the likes of him ruin your day." Ginger glanced about before adding, "Is Charles not with you?"

"No, he was called to work." With a forced laugh, she continued. "That part hasn't changed much since London. What about Basil?"

Linking Felicia's arm in hers, Ginger said, "He's up to his ears in Miss Graves' case. I'm not unsympathetic to the poor girl's demise, but I'd rather hoped our time in Amsterdam would be a family holiday. But at least I have you. Shall we take in the last of the dressage competition?"

Brushing Ginger off would make her more inquisitive, and Felicia was no stranger to Ginger's astute observation and keen deduction skills. "I should like that."

Later, when Felicia finally made it back to her flat, Charles was there, waiting.

"I can't believe, amid hundreds of people," Felicia began once they were alone in the sitting room, "that she saw me with Bottomley there. What are the chances?"

Charles held her gaze but said nothing.

Felicia shrunk under his stare, under his look of . . .what? Disappointment in her apparent lack of spy skills? Regret that he'd agreed to admit her into his secret world?

Charles caressed her arm, his eyes softening. "Don't be too hard on yourself, love. The unbelievable and the unexpected happen all the time in this business. The main thing is you were able to think on your feet." Charles gave her a comforting squeeze. "Bottomley comes across as a bull in a China shop and could very likely have bumped into a lady and stamped on her feet."

Gripping the rope of pearls around her neck, Felicia slumped into a chair. "I just don't want to fail on my first assignment, Charles. What will they do if they think me unfit?"

Charles sat beside her and took her hand. "They wouldn't have agreed to let you take this on if they thought that. Remember your training, Felicia. You excelled in every aspect."

"But that was make-believe. This is real."

"And it will get more real." Charles held her gaze. "Are you sure you want to continue? This life isn't for everyone."

Felicia stiffened. She'd wanted this so badly, wanted what Charles had so badly; she'd thrown every ounce of her being into becoming the perfect spy. She excelled at learning Dutch, was surprisingly adept at self-defence tactics, and had studied maps and secret codes. She'd even learned to fire a pistol, hitting the bull's-eye nearly every time.

Why was she losing her nerve at something as

benign as being caught arguing with a fellow agent, a man known by Ginger as the British journalist Ernest Bottomley?

Was it because she had been untruthful with Ginger?

Ginger was Felicia's closest thing to a sister, and she was her dearest friend. The lie had caught in her throat like dry bread.

Or was it because someone had died? And not only someone but the person she and Charles had been tasked to watch.

"Have we failed Nora Graves, Charles?"

"Darling? No one suspected that her life was in danger in any way. We weren't expected to tail her twenty-four hours a day. We rightly assumed she was tucked up in bed safely for the night. Besides, her death appears to be entirely unrelated to her sister."

The sister was their real target.

"Oh, Charles, do you think someone killed Nora to draw out Esther?"

Charles frowned. "I suppose that's possible. We'll have to wait for the autopsy report. If the cause of death is suspicious, we may have our answer. Now, what did Bottomley know?"

"Nothing." Felicia pouted. "At least not anything he was prepared to tell me. Honestly, he treats me like a child, as if the two of us talking together in public would expose us to the world."

"I wouldn't take it personally," Charles said. "I don't think he likes women, particularly strong women."

"Unfortunately," Felicia added with a sigh, "he's not alone in that."

CHAPTER SEVENTEEN

A message arrived the next morning from Inspector Van der Meer. Ginger perked up as Basil opened the note. "What does it say?"

"The autopsy on Miss Graves is complete."

"And?"

Basil sipped his tea. "Water was found in her lungs."

"She drowned."

"And she had a significant amount of succinylcholine in her system."

"That's a poison arrow derivative, isn't it?"

Basil nodded.

Ginger slumped back in her chair. "It's murder, then?"

"Yes, love." Basil stared over the rim of his glass. "It's murder."

"What do you want to do now?"

"Have you got any ideas?"

"I'm assuming the poison was injected?"

Basil's hazel eyes dropped back to the note. "The pinprick Dr. Jansen found confirms that."

Ginger leaned forward. "You might recall that I met the veterinarian working at the Olympic stables, Mr. KIaassen, when I last called in to see Scout."

"Yes, you mentioned that was where you first spoke to Miss Hughes."

"Exactly. Scout was grooming Miss Hughes' horse. Afterwards, when I was alone with Mr. KIaassen, he showed signs of confusion whilst going through his supplies. One of his syringes was missing. He said he keeps precise records of everything—medication, surgical supplies, etcetera—so that he'll never be caught short."

"I can see why," Basil said. "When you're in charge of keeping animals of great value healthy and alive. A disgruntled owner could sue him for everything he's worth."

"I didn't make much of it at the time, but now . . . I don't know."

"Well, there is a connection between Mr. KIaassen and Miss Graves."

"Ah, yes," Ginger said. "Miss Hughes is boycotting the athletics but has a horse in the Games. And we mustn't forget about her rider, Bernard Masters."

"What about him?" Basil asked. "Did he know Miss Graves as well?"

"That I don't know, but he behaves rather abrasively

towards both Miss Hughes and Mr. Klaassen. I just find it peculiar."

They called at the nurses' station at the Olympic stadium before heading to the stables. The head nurse, dressed in the usual white frock with a white identifying cap pinned on the top of her head, stared back with tired eyes. In English, she responded to Basil's introduction and his odd query.

"No, sir. We wouldn't have a missing syringe as we're not set up to give injections. We carry bandages, splints, headache pills—that kind of thing. Serious injuries are transported to the hospital by ambulance."

"If one were to be in the market for a syringe," Ginger started, "for whatever reason, where would one go for that?"

"One's doctor, I suspect. The only reason I can think of that a patient would need a syringe without his doctor's care would be if he was diabetic. Insulin is available in those circumstances."

Ginger glanced at Basil. Insulin was indeed a miracle discovery for those afflicted by diabetes, but this malaise didn't seem to be a concern in this particular case.

"Thank you for your time, nurse," Basil said.

Their next stop was the stables. Just as their taxicab pulled up, another pulled away with Bernard Masters travelling alone in the back.

The stables were abuzz with those attending either the horses or the grounds. Ginger's eyes lit up when she found Scout sweeping out the stalls. He was turning into a capable and handsome young man.

"Mum." Scout's eyes darted about before returning his gaze to Ginger. He kicked the dirt with one boot and said, "You don't have to check on me every day."

"As it turns out, I'm here to see Mr. KIaassen. And besides, your father hasn't seen the stables yet."

"Hello, Dad," Scout said, his cheeks rosy after Ginger's mild chastisement.

"Son," Basil said with a smile. "How are things in the stables? Are you enjoying your Olympic experience?"

"Very much. Mr. Masters has been under the weather, so I've been taking Pegasus out on his jumps."

"You're jumping with him?" Ginger asked incredulously.

"I've jumped plenty at school. Miss Hughes thinks I'm doing a fine job of it."

"I'm sure you are," Basil said. "And well done, my boy. But we do need to speak to Mr. KIaassen on official business."

Scout's eyes grew round. "Do you need to talk to him about Nora Graves, the lady athlete who drowned? Everyone's been gabbing about her. She was British, wasn't she?"

Ginger held in the sigh threatening to release. She did her best to shield her children from the dark side of the work she and Basil did, but with Scout, it had grown increasingly difficult to do so.

"Sadly, Miss Graves has passed away," Basil said. "The details of her death are still under investigation."

"Mr. KIaassen is in his office," Scout said. "At least that was where he was the last I saw him."

Ginger circled Pegasus Pride with Scout and whispered in her son's ear once obscured by the horse's great flank. "Remember how I used to give you little jobs?"

Before Scout had become a member of the family, he lived in East London with an ailing uncle and his older cousin, though, mostly, the lad was unsupervised. Scout had proven himself useful on the SS *Rosa*, and these small tasks had been a way for Ginger to give him money he was too proud to take as a gift. Over the years, Scout had eagerly joined Ginger on certain cases, and now she needed help with this one.

"Mum? What do you want me to do?"

"Keep a close eye on Mr. Masters. Let me know if you find out anything out of the ordinary."

Scout's eyes narrowed as he nodded slowly. "All right. Mr. Masters is a good rider, but I don't like him."

"He's a brash man, but that doesn't make him guilty of anything," Ginger said. "I just want to make sure. Report back if you learn anything of interest."

"What were you two conspiring about?" Basil asked when Ginger joined him.

"Oh, just horse and rider issues."

After strolling through the corridor past the stalls and equipment rooms, they arrived at Mr. KIaassen's office just as he was locking up and about to leave. "Oh, hello, Mrs. Reed." His eyes landed on Basil.

"Hello, Mr. KIaassen," Ginger returned. "This is my husband, Chief Inspector Basil Reed of Scotland Yard. Inspector Van der Meer has asked him to be a consultant on Nora Graves' case."

Mr. KIaassen clicked his tongue. "I've heard the news. It's much talked about amongst the athletes for one of their own to suffer such a fate during what is supposed to be a joyous time. It's such a shame."

"Indeed," Basil said.

The veterinarian's eyes, looking larger through his spectacles, moved between Ginger and Basil. "I don't know how I can help the police. The equestrian and track and field competitions don't overlap. I've never spoken to anyone associated with the athletics, aside from Miss Hughes."

Ginger found it interesting how often Marion Hughes' name came up. "Is Miss Hughes on the grounds?"

"She called on me yesterday to arrange to have Pegasus Pride shipped back to England as soon as he's finished competing."

"Is she not travelling with him?" Ginger asked.

"She's leaving Amsterdam," Mr. KIaassen said. "A bit earlier than she first planned."

It seemed a bit too convenient to Ginger that Miss Hughes would change her plans like that, miss her horse and rider's final competition unless she had a reason to get out of the spotlight.

"Mr. KIaassen," Basil started, "it's been determined that Miss Graves' death wasn't accidental."

The man's jaw dropped. "Are you saying she was murdered?"

Basil nodded. "Poison was found in her system, and it appears to have been injected."

"If you recall," Ginger began, "yesterday when I was here, you thought you had misplaced a syringe. Did you ever find it?"

"Oh, I understand now." Mr. KIaassen's finger went to his chin as he shook his head. "No, I have not." His gaze shot to Basil. "Do you think someone stole my syringe? To commit *murder?*"

"We can't know that for sure until the syringe in question is located," Basil said. "Who has access to your supplies?"

"Well, I keep them locked in my office, but . . ."

"But?" Ginger prodded gently.

"Well, I found my office door unlocked a few days ago. I always lock it. It's a well-engrained habit, but there was a distraction—and I left it unlocked for a short while."

"What was the distraction?" Ginger asked. "Whoever intended to raid your office could've been responsible for it."

"A horse became agitated. He had picked up a burr."

"How likely is that?" Ginger asked. "In this stable?"

Mr. KIaassen pushed up on his spectacles. "Not very."

"So was it deliberate?" Basil asked. "Do you have any idea who might be responsible for that?"

"No," Mr. KIaassen said. "It could've been anyone, if it was anyone. A burr is a burr. It happens."

"Thank you for your time, Mr. KIaassen," Basil said.

The veterinarian disappeared into one of the stalls.

"Mum!"

Ginger tugged on Basil's arm again, away from the stable, not wanting to be seen.

She was slightly out of breath when they reached Scout. "Have you found something already?"

Scout held out a notebook.

"What's this?" Basil asked.

Ginger opened the journal and scoured the contents. "This belongs to Bernard Masters."

Scout shoved his fists into his trouser pockets. "It must've fallen out of his pocket as he was leaving."

Ginger bit her lip. Perhaps the notebook had fallen, though Scout had learned a thing or two about pickpocketing when he lived on the streets. Best not to get too focused on the details at the moment.

Basil frowned. "What is it?"

Ginger pointed at the entries, eager to distract Basil. "A row of numbers and a row of initials. These sums appear regularly each month, with the same initials." She arched a brow at Basil. "Do you think he's blackmailing people?"

"That's a crime, to be sure, but it doesn't necessarily connect him with our murder."

Ginger's finger paused over the initials. NG. "Nora Graves? And look here, MH and GC."

"Marion Hughes?" Basil postulated. "If we're looking at people in Masters' circle."

"That could include Gerrit KIaassen, which would explain the frosty relations between him and Bernard Masters. Perhaps Nora Graves refused to pay or couldn't pay."

"Perhaps, but that doesn't explain the letter from Dankworth."

"Is it possible two things were going on at once?" Ginger proposed. "Mr. Dankworth's pursuit of love and Mr. Masters' pursuit of blackmail money."

Basil conceded, "I suppose we could wait for this rider to return and have a word. But don't think my cooperation has absolved either of you. We'll discuss this when we get back to London."

Ginger smiled covertly at Scout. "You'd better get back to work. I'm sure Pegasus Pride is missing you."

Taking Basil's hand, Ginger headed for an exit at the back of the stables. The way he squeezed hers confirmed that his anger had seeped away. Perhaps they should take time for a walk and enjoy each other's company. With everything that had been going on, they hadn't had much time to spend alone.

Before she could suggest such an outing, terse voices brought them to a standstill, both female, one with a crisp English and the other a latent Continental accent. Neither was speaking loudly enough for whole sentences to be heard, but individual words drifted their way.

Gone.

Dead.

Lie.

If a woman hadn't been murdered, Ginger would've considered the conversation to be none of her business, but she recognised the voice of the English woman. Marion Hughes.

Ginger nodded towards a knothole and carefully stepped through the hay to the stable wall—after all, she had to consider her Italian leather T-strap shoes. The hole was low and easier for Ginger to bend to peek through quickly. Marion Hughes had her back to her, blocking the view of the other woman.

The other woman said, "I will find out who killed her, and I will kill them!"

"I don't know what you're shouting at me for," Miss Hughes said. "I had nothing to do with it."

"She told me you didn't like her."

Miss Hughes scoffed. "I'm *sure* I wasn't the only one."

A quick slap to the face was the other woman's response. Shocked, Ginger held her breath not only from the sudden violence but because, when Miss Hughes held her cheek and turned, the face of the foreign woman came into view.

Edith Smythe. The crescent-shaped scar on her forearm proved it.

Ginger had spent time training Miss Smythe during the Great War. Later, the woman was discovered to be a double agent and was wanted by several countries for war crimes.

Miss Smythe had been aggressive and fearless then. Her eyes flashed like a wildcat, her anger barely restrained. She was definitely dangerous now.

CHAPTER EIGHTEEN

"Quick!" Ginger said, pulling on Basil's arm. Moving out of one stall, down the corridor, and around the bend to the stalls that shared a wall took longer than one might like. By the time Ginger and Basil had reached the one Ginger had been spying on, the foreign woman had fled. Only Miss Hughes was there, her abused cheek a bright red. She stared at Ginger and Basil's sudden arrival with alarm.

"Wh—what on earth?" she sputtered.

"Who were you just speaking with?" Ginger demanded. "We heard you through the wall on the other side. She's a dangerous woman."

"If you know she's dangerous, then you know who she is." Miss Hughes braced her hands on her hips.

"But who is she to you?" Ginger pressed.

At Miss Hughes' seeming reluctance to answer, Basil said, "Miss Hughes, please answer the question."

MURDER AT THE OLYMPICS

"She's a mad woman. Nora's sister."

Ginger was surprised at the answer. "Her sister?"

"That's what she said. I don't know her name other than that." She waved a hand in exasperation. "But I can tell you she's very upset about Nora's accident."

"That's the thing," Basil said. "The authorities no longer believe Miss Graves' death to be accidental. She was murdered."

Miss Hughes stilled. "Oh. That's rather unnerving, isn't it? Why would someone want to kill Nora?"

"We're hoping you can help us with that question, Miss Hughes," Basil answered.

"How can I be of help?" Miss Hughes asked. "I really am very busy. Besides, I've already told the police everything I know."

"Not everything," Ginger said. "You never mentioned your jealousy concerning Nora Graves' relationship with Mr. Dankworth or your own strong feelings for him."

"So?" Miss Hughes returned petulantly.

Ginger inclined her head. "It gives you motive."

Miss Hughes' eyes flashed with anger. She spoke loudly, drawing the attention of others in the stable. "It's not a secret that I didn't care for Nora or her immoral relationship with Claude, but that doesn't mean I hurt her."

"Miss Hughes, are you being blackmailed by your rider, Mr. Masters?"

Stunned by the question and the sudden change in

topic, Miss Hughes' mouth dropped. "Bernard is a rotten blighter."

"Did he know Nora Graves?"

Miss Hughes laughed. "Nora's not the sweet victim that you think she is. There's a reason she stayed in the races, and it wasn't because she felt the British women were making a mistake by boycotting the event."

"Then why?" Ginger asked.

Miss Hughes cocked her head. "Because she needed the money."

"How can she make money by competing at the Olympics when the athletes aren't paid?"

"This might come as a surprise to you, Mrs. Reed, but folks like to bet on sports."

"She was under pressure to stay in the race because bets were being placed," Ginger said, understanding. "I'm assuming she would've benefited as well."

"Not as much as you would think."

"Why do you think she needed the money?" Ginger pressed. "To pay off her blackmailer?"

Miss Hughes shrugged. "That's none of my business."

"You know what I think," Ginger said. "I think you and your rider are working the scheme together. Perhaps Mr. Masters did it for the money, but you did it for the power. And when Miss Graves refused, you threatened to kill her."

"Nonsense and poppycock!"

"Perhaps you didn't mean for Nora to die, and maybe you weren't the one who pushed her, but now you're an accomplice."

Miss Hughes jumped to her feet. "I won't be treated this way!"

"Miss Hughes," Basil said with authority, "perhaps it would be better if we discussed this at the police station. We'd have more privacy."

"I don't care a hoot about privacy, Mr. Reed."

"It's Chief Inspector Reed," Basil said sternly. "And I'm afraid I'm not making a request. Would you rather I arrest you here? It would make a quick return to England quite impossible."

Miss Hughes made a fist and stamped her feet like an overgrown child. "Do you know who my family is?"

"Indeed I do," Basil answered. "The Hughes from Leicestershire. And I'm afraid no one is above the law, especially when it comes to murder."

Miss Hughes' eye twitched, and her lower lip trembled. Ginger felt a twinge of pity for her. It was particularly difficult for people used to getting their own way to have to submit to the authority and rights of others.

"Miss Hughes," Ginger said gently. "It's just a time to talk. I'll be there too. We can have coffee together, and you can tell us your side of the story."

After a deep breath, Miss Hughes relented. "Very well. I could use a coffee about now."

Basil shot Ginger a look of appreciation. Neither of them would relish the thought of wrestling down a distraught woman and dragging her to the police station.

CHAPTER NINETEEN

Accompanied by Ginger and Marion Hughes, Basil entered the main door of the central police station. The front desk clerk immediately approached. With his eyes on Basil, he asked in English, "Are you Chief Inspector Reed?"

"Yes?" Basil said.

"Inspector Van der Meer would like to see you immediately. He's in his office."

Ginger turned to Marion Hughes. "Let's go and find that coffee."

Basil gave Ginger a nod of appreciation, then knocked on the office door marked Hoofdinspecteur Van der Meer.

Heavily decorated in dark wood—desk, chair, wall panelling—the room had a distinctly masculine feel. The odour of cigar and cigarette smoke hung in the air.

Basil sat in a chair facing the inspector's cluttered desk, which was lit by a green banker's lamp.

"Good day," Inspector Van der Meer said. "I'm glad you found your way to me." He withdrew a pair of thin cotton gloves from a desk drawer, carefully slipping them on. Then, deliberately, he opened a small rectangular box, its brass clasp clicking softly. Inside, nestled on a clean white linen cloth, was a metal syringe of the type used on cattle or other large animals, like horses. Basil leaned in slightly, his eyes keenly observing the syringe while respecting its untouched state. The careful handling by Van der Meer underscored the potential significance of every print, every mark on its metallic surface.

"It was retrieved from the Wilgenbocht Canal, not far from where the body was found." Van der Meer picked up the syringe and held it with the fingertips of both hands so Basil could get a good look.

"Our men had spread the word amongst the fishermen along the canals to be on the lookout for anything suspicious and to report it to the police immediately. This was snagged in a fishing line early this morning."

"Perhaps it's the break we were both hoping for," Basil said.

Inspector Van der Meer nodded his agreement. "It's been carefully preserved for analysis. Dried of water now, but a small amount of liquid remains in the barrel."

"Let me guess," Basil said. "It has no colouring and no odour."

"Much clearer-looking than the canal water itself," Inspector Van der Meer said as he placed the syringe back in the box. "My guess is a poison, but we shall wait for the report from the laboratory."

Poison made sense to Basil. There was, of course, the chance this was a syringe used for veterinary purposes and someone had simply thrown it into the canal. However, there wasn't any farmland near the area where the body had been found. And given the pinprick found on the body, it seemed more likely that they were looking at the murder weapon.

"What about fingerprints?" Basil asked.

"Yes, that is trickier. It's been in the water for a while, but even so, it might still reveal something of the hand that wielded it."

"It's all moot if our killer hasn't been arrested before and has no fingerprints on file." Basil pushed up from his chair. "I have Miss Marion Hughes in the interview room with Mrs. Reed."

"Miss Hughes, the horse owner?"

"The very one."

"I don't suppose you saw the write-up in your London paper by a Mr. Bottomley, did you?"

Basil shook his head, and the inspector produced the paper, opening it to a particular article. The headline read: *Miss Hughes Swallows Pride and Leaves with Horse's Tail between Legs.* The story continued with an unflattering retelling of Pegasus Pride's performance in the dressage competition and shaming Britain for not gaining a medal in what should have been the country's strongest showing. Ginger had thought Masters had done well in the event, but she hadn't seen the final results.

Basil frowned. "Why do you suppose Bottomley has it in for Miss Hughes?"

"I was hoping you would know," Inspector Van der Meer said. "As a man with connections with the British government."

"I'm afraid I don't understand."

"We have good reason to believe that your Mr. Bottomley, if that's even his real name, is a spy."

Basil snorted. *That obtuse little man was a suspected spy?* "Surely, you jest."

"I'm afraid not, Chief Inspector. He's a spy, and from what I hear, not one of the good ones."

GINGER STAYED BEHIND in the interview room with Marion Hughes. She had promised Miss Hughes a coffee, after all. Basil had obtained permission from Inspector Van der Meer for her to do so and had promised her that he and the inspector wouldn't be long.

The interview room held a single table and four chairs. The white walls were unadorned. An officer brought two coffees, sweetened with milk and sugar, and left them alone. Miss Hughes' anger and sense of effrontery had deflated into despondency, her eyes portraying a childlike wounding. The two women sipped in silence. Ginger savoured the peace and quiet. It gave her time to think about the foreign woman and the shock she had felt at seeing her again.

"How long do I have to stay here?"

Miss Hughes' voice pulled Ginger out of her reverie. "I'm not sure. Once Chief Inspector Reed returns, we'll know."

Using what seemed to be a favoured phrase, Miss Hughes repeated, "This is all such nonsense and poppycock."

"Why don't you finish your coffee? I'm sure he'll be here by then."

"Fine. If you give me a cigarette."

"I don't have a cigarette on me," Ginger said, "but I'll ask the officer in the corridor. After sticking her head out the door, Ginger returned with the requested cigarette, a box of matches, and an ashtray.

As they waited, Ginger's mind returned to France during the last year of the Great War. In her mind, she saw a dilapidated-looking farmhouse—a façade to keep anyone who might've wandered off the beaten path from investigating further. Beyond the wooden door on broken hinges was another door, securely locked. The property interfaced with the forest, thick trees, and brush that also kept the training outdoors hidden.

Ginger had worked as a secret service agent for the

British government for four years, work that she'd kept secret from her first husband, Daniel, Lord Gold, who'd been serving on the front lines. Captain Smithwick—just thinking about the man made Ginger's blood run cold—had told her she was ready to train up-and-coming spies and that the females amongst them needed to know how to defend themselves physically. Ginger had become adept at such techniques and was eager to teach them to others.

All the girls had been initially timid, if not determined to learn, but one stood out in Ginger's memory. A woman Ginger knew as Edith Smythe, undoubtedly not her real name. Edith had a ferocious tenacity, an animalistic drive, and a reputation for being fearless. The other girls feared her and resisted training with her. Ginger, wanting to encourage the others to face Edith—as a male attacker could be equally dangerous—went up against Edith herself.

Ginger immediately understood why the others were afraid. Edith, armed with a dummy knife, was poised to attack. Her mandate was to get Ginger in a compromising position where Ginger would have to surrender or die in a real-case scenario. As the agent under attack, Ginger needed to relieve Edith of the weapon and reverse the situation.

Edith's eyes shone with intent, and Ginger had the fleeting thought that her student wanted to outwit the teacher. However, Ginger had the advantage of experience. She danced with Edith, staying just out of reach when the woman thrust the knife in her direction. To the group, she explained, "Don't focus on the knife alone. Keep your opponent in reach, but never near enough to strike."

Edith had taken that moment to rush Ginger, growling as she lunged. Ginger took a swift step to the side, sharply blocking Edith, setting her off balance slightly. This split second gave Ginger the upper hand, and she grabbed Edith's wrist, twisting it until the knife fell to the ground.

"My turn." Ginger picked up the knife, holding it backwards in her fist as if she would stab a table, and instinctively sliced the air in front of her. Edith's lack of experience showed as she failed to jerk out of the way, and the knife caught the inside of her wrist. Blood splattered everywhere. The knife had been a dummy, but the edge was sharp enough to tear the delicate skin of the inner wrist.

Ginger would never forget how Edith stared back at her with horrified disbelief. Ginger immediately ripped off a strip of her underskirt and wrapped it around Edith's wrist before rushing her to get it treated by the doctor on site. Because of Ginger's quick thinking, little blood was lost, but the slash was deep enough to merit stitches.

Edith had returned to her training under Ginger's tutelage but hadn't let the injury, which eventually had stretched into a crescent-shaped scar, slow her down.

Ginger was brought back to the moment by Miss

Hughes' heavy sigh. "I'm actually glad you and your husband showed up when you did."

"Oh?"

"Nora's sister, she was so angry." Miss Hughes' hand went to her face where Edith had slapped her. "I thought she was going to kill me."

"I'm assuming the elder Miss Graves came to Amsterdam to meet up with her sister," Ginger said. "Did you ever see the two of them together?"

"No." Miss Hughes tapped ash into the ashtray. "But . . . perhaps that was why Nora sneaked out. To meet her sister."

"Why would she do that in the middle of the night?" Ginger countered, though, since she was a double agent wanted by several governments, Ginger could understand Edith's need for a covert meeting.

There was also the letter from Mr. Dankworth drawing Miss Graves out that Ginger had to consider. As believable as Mr. Dankworth's story was, that he wanted to repair their fractured love affair, he remained a credible suspect in Ginger's mind.

After sipping the last of her coffee, Ginger asked, "Why did you decide to go back to England earlier than planned, Miss Hughes?"

Miss Hughes flung her hands in the air. "I'm tired of all the drama. Bernard has abandoned us, me and Pegasus, and without a rider, I see no reason to remain."

Ginger felt a twinge of alarm. "Mr. Masters has left Holland?"

"Yes. He was exceptionally agitated when he told me. And we still have one competition left; I could kill the man!" At Ginger's questioning look, she added, "That's a figure of speech. I've never killed anyone."

Finally, Basil and the inspector returned from their excursion. Ginger looked eagerly at her husband. "Is there any news?"

Before Basil could answer, Inspector Van der Meer turned to Marion Hughes. "Miss Hughes, you're under arrest for the murder of Miss Nora Graves."

CHAPTER TWENTY

In London, at the end of a long day, Ginger and Basil often retreated to the sitting room at Hartigan House and enjoyed a brandy together whilst sharing the details of what had transpired for them over the previous eight to ten hours.

As they were in Amsterdam, they enjoyed that moment of relaxation seated at a candle-lit table overlooking one of the canals. The moonlight glistened like jewels only a mythical creature could collect.

Mr. Bottomley's scathing report on Mr. Masters and Pegasus Pride—it seemed the journalist could write no other kinds of reports—came up.

"Apparently, Mr. Masters had a small stumble, costing them points," Ginger explained. "And he lost a chance at a medal. Perhaps that was the reason he left so dramatically."

"Emotions run high in sporting events." Basil

MURDER AT THE OLYMPICS

poured one finger of brandy from a crystal decanter into two crystal glasses. "Especially at this level."

"It wasn't a great day for Miss Hughes," Ginger said. "Her sudden arrest by Inspector Van der Meer was rather dramatic."

"The evidence against Miss Hughes is rather damning," Basil said as he handed one glass to Ginger. "She was heard threatening Nora Graves by one of their American counterparts, Charlotte Hartley. Dankworth's testimony that Miss Hughes badgered him and Miss Graves is supported by other women on the British ladies' athletic team. A telegram from Scotland Yard came today stating that three of the athletes had been questioned, at my request, and support the coach's claims. Miss Hughes shared a room with Miss Graves, so the probability that she saw Dankworth's letter written to Miss Graves to rendezvous the night of her murder was high, and she made sudden changes to her plans to leave Amsterdam earlier than she had intended."

"You make a good case, but we've both seen situations where the most likely suspect didn't end up being the killer. We don't know if Miss Graves shared the same feelings for Mr. Dankworth as he had for her. Perhaps she did, but her feelings could've changed, and he mightn't have been accepting of an end to the relationship." Ginger sipped her brandy. "I find it interesting that Miss Hartley's name has come into play as evidence against Miss Hughes. When I spoke to her, she didn't hide that she thought poorly about Brits in general and disparaged Miss Graves for not boycotting the Olympics with the rest of her team."

"I see," Basil said. "She might be attempting to frame Miss Hughes. I'll take it into consideration."

"Then there are those ghastly journalists whose reports on the eight hundred metres were close to character assassinations. In particular, that American, Jack Montrose."

"Another long shot." Basil lifted his glass.

"And what about Bernard Masters, running off so suddenly?"

"I contacted the Yard, and they're looking for him. We'll get him if he's guilty of blackmailing."

"We can't overlook his connection with Nora Graves."

"Indeed we can't. I've asked for a check on her finances, and there appears to be a weekly withdrawal from her bank account for the same amount listed by her initials in Masters' notebook."

Ginger waved her fingers. "There you go."

"Blackmail doesn't necessarily lead to murder." Basil sipped his drink, then added, "Ginger, love, you seem determined to find Miss Hughes innocent. Is there something you're not telling me?"

As her mind raced, Ginger pushed red strands of her hair behind her ears. How often, in the last few years, had she found herself in the tricky situation of having information that could help the police but also put her in the position of having to skirt around her vow of secrecy to the Crown? She was fed up with it!

"That woman Miss Hughes was cross with at the stables," she started reluctantly. "I met her, briefly, in the war."

Basil's left eyebrow shot up. Ginger knew he suspected her involvement with the secret service. *How can he not?* And how silly she couldn't just come out and say it. It was the one barrier in their marriage, the only thing that Ginger didn't give to Basil, the only thing she continually held back.

Yet, Basil never pushed her. He, of all people, knew the rules. You couldn't rise to the position of chief inspector at Scotland Yard and not encounter government agents, even if it meant being constantly frustrated by their tight lips.

"What *can* you tell me?" he asked, as if proving her assumptions about him.

"She's dangerous."

"What did she have to do with Marion Hughes?"

"Miss Hughes told me that she claimed to be Nora Graves' elder sister."

Basil whistled. "What name did you know her by?"

"Edith Smythe."

Basil sighed. "The deeper I get into the investigation, the more I'm seeing that this isn't a run-of-the-mill murder."

Ginger sipped her brandy, then said, "I've come to that conclusion myself."

"I have an interesting titbit to share as well," Basil said. "Inspector Van der Meer's connections have unearthed their own information. It turns out the jolly Mr. Bottomley isn't who we think he is either."

Ginger inclined her head. "He's not a journalist for *The Daily Picture*?"

"Perhaps he is, but it's not his primary job, according to Van der Meer. Apparently, Bottomley is a spy."

Ginger slowly blinked as Basil kept his gaze latched on her, no doubt trying to read her reaction. Calmly, she said, "That seems rather extreme."

"But not out of the realm of possibility."

"Why could he be spying?" Ginger asked with sincerity. "Or should I say, on whom? Miss Graves?"

"That would be the question of the day," Basil said. "But whatever the case, Van der Meer made it clear that Bottomley wasn't a man who could be trusted. Not by us, nor apparently, the British government."

Ginger worked her lips. Having met the disagreeable man herself, she didn't doubt Basil's statement or the inspector's concern.

More troubling to her was Felicia and that row she'd had with Bottomley. As much as Ginger would like to believe it was a coincidental encounter, Felicia's strange behaviour of late brought it into question. Ginger's heart sank.

. . .

The next day, Ginger intercepted Felicia as the latter was leaving her flat.

"Felicia, darling!"

Felicia turned, a glimpse of surprise registering on her face before melting into nonchalance.

Ginger was an expert at the move, having practiced it thousands of times. The Felicia she knew was not. Or at least, she never used to be.

The Felicia Ginger knew wore her feelings on her sleeves; her emotions etched on her face. Ginger never worried about not knowing if Felicia was happy or sad, worried or ecstatic, amused or angered.

This new Felicia was unnerving.

"Ginger? This is unexpected."

"Basil was called away," Ginger said casually, "and I thought I'd chance coming over to see if you were at home. It looks like I'm catching you at a bad time. Or can you spare an hour to go for tea?"

Felicia hesitated for a split second before smiling. "Of course. I'd love to." Linking her arm with Ginger's, she added, "I must see my favourite sister-friend as much as possible while she's here."

They went to an outdoor café on a narrow cobblestoned street, shaded nicely by the tall shops and residences surrounding it.

"You seem very happy, Felicia."

Felicia stared up over her lashes. "More than usual?"

"I'd say so."

"I suppose I am. As they say, a little change can do one wonders."

"A sense of purpose, perhaps?"

Felicia stared back. "I think one needs a purpose, don't you? A reason to get up in the mornings?"

Ginger held Felicia's grey-eyed gaze. "And you've found that purpose here, have you?"

"I suppose I have."

"And it's more than being a superb wife to Charles?"

"Ginger, what is this line of questioning? Is something the matter? Are you cross that I've left Grandmama in your care? I gather you miss the diversion I offered."

Ginger smiled, thinking she was quite impressed with the diversion Felicia was attempting *now*. She leaned in. "We're sisters and good friends, as you say, so I won't beat around the bush. Are you working *with* Charles?"

Felicia sputtered. "Whatever do you mean? It's not like they'll let a woman step into the House of Lords."

"This is Holland. The House doesn't sit here."

"Charles isn't so busy here either. Which is why I'm happier."

"Did you know Mr. Bottomley, the journalist you 'bumped' into yesterday, is a spy?"

"How would I know such a thing?" She wrinkled her nose. "How do *you* know such a thing?"

"Inspector Van de Meer relayed the news to Basil."

"Oh?" Felicia glanced away before asking, "What are the police planning to do with such information?"

Ginger raised a thinly plucked brow. "Perhaps Charles knows the answer to that."

"I wouldn't know."

"Are you *certain* about that?"

"Again, I don't know what you mean."

"I think you know *exactly* what I mean."

Felicia frowned. "It seems that sisters don't tell each other everything." Her gaze had been on her coffee but latched on to Ginger's eyes. "Do they?"

"Have you answered my question?"

"If I have, it wasn't my intention. *You,* of all people, should know that wouldn't be possible."

Oh mercy.

Clearly, Felicia knew about Ginger's work with the secret service, but how much did she know? And how deeply was Felicia in the organisation?

Ginger swallowed. "It's a dangerous game, Felicia. Frankly, I'm disappointed in Charles."

"You mustn't blame him. I figured things out on my own, you see. I'm not just a silly flapper girl after all."

"I never thought you were."

"And it was I who insisted on joining, er, *the game*, as you put it."

"I really wish you hadn't," Ginger said sincerely. "I'll not sleep a wink now, knowing it."

"Put it out of your mind, Ginger. Besides, we're in peacetime. The stakes are low, comparatively."

Ginger hoped Felicia was right about that. Yet, poor Nora Graves, lying dead in the mortuary, was proof that spy work at any time in history could be a dangerous affair.

By the time Ginger returned to her hotel, she was exhausted. She found mind games to be as taxing as physical endurance. What she needed was a good long soak in the bath while sipping bubbly water and reading a Lord Peter Wimsey mystery. She checked at the front desk in case there were any messages from home. The clerk handed her a blank envelope.

It wasn't from England, which eased Ginger's mind. *No news is good news.*

However, tension returned in a flurry as she read the short missive.

I know who the killer is. Meet me at Vondelpark on the benches by the Joost van den Vondel statue at two p.m. sharp. Come alone, or you won't find me.

Edith

CHAPTER TWENTY-ONE

If Ginger was going to make it on time, she'd have to leave immediately, with no chance to tell Basil about it, especially since she didn't know where he was. The best she could do was to send a message to the police station and hope for the best.

The hotel rooms conveniently provided paper and envelopes for guests, and Ginger quickly jotted out the letter's contents, adding: It's a public place, so don't worry. The front desk clerk assured her he'd immediately see to its delivery, reassuring Ginger by calling for a pageboy.

She quickly dressed in a simple violet day dress trimmed with a matching fabric belt, slipped into a pair of black leather pumps, and plopped a summer cloche on her head.

As the taxicab traversed the busy streets of Amsterdam, Ginger barely registered the passing landmarks, her heart thrumming at the prospect of seeing the woman she knew as Edith Smythe after all these years.

More troubling was that Edith Smythe knew that Ginger was in Amsterdam and the hotel where she and Basil were staying. The woman must've seen Ginger at the stables, too, and recognised her. Finding her hotel was child's play for a savvy agent like Edith Smythe. Ginger was at a disadvantage, having just learned about Nora Graves.

What had Nora Grave's elder sister been up to for the past ten years? She had hoodwinked the British government regarding her loyalty to the Crown. She'd been in hiding, but where? On the Continent? Here in Holland?

She must've understood the danger that that could bring to Nora. How despairing it must be for her to think she had had a hand in her sister's death.

The hairs on the back of Ginger's neck stood. She had the inexplicable feeling that her taxicab was being followed. Who would follow her? As far as the world knew, and everyone in Amsterdam, Ginger had come to watch the Games. And that was true! She had come simply to watch the Games.

As a precaution, Ginger told her driver to let her out at the park's gate.

Vondelpark was a massive area. According to the sign at one of the entrances, it was nearly fifty hectares or one hundred and twenty acres. Ginger was glad Edith had been precise about the meeting place.

Spotting the Joost van den Vondel statue commemorating a beloved Dutch writer for whom the park was named, Ginger checked her wristwatch. She had five minutes to spare.

The park was a grand landscape architectural design of large green lawns and tall leafy trees crisscrossed with pristine walking paths. Man-made ponds and fountains, like the one Ginger now waited at, created soothing water attractions. Many people milled about enjoying the pleasant atmosphere: couples strolling arm in arm, mothers or nannies pushing babies in prams, and families picnicking.

A woman dressed in a pale blue day dress strolled by Ginger, staring straight ahead, not making eye contact. Ginger recognised her right away. Her shoulders, slender as always, scooped forward, and circles had formed under puffy eyes. A grieving soul if there ever was one.

The woman took a seat on a bench that backed against another bench about twenty feet away.

Just as Ginger was about to make her way to that back-facing bench, she was intercepted.

"Mrs. Reed!"

What rotten luck! That despicable American journalist, Jack Montrose, stepped in front of her, blocking her view of Miss Graves.

"I've heard about Nora Graves and your husband consulting with the Dutch police. Do you care to comment?"

"I do not."

"Is the case closed now that an arrest has been made?"

"Excuse me, Mr. Montrose, but this really is a bad time."

"No one has shared the cause of death. Do you know?"

"Mr. Montrose, please."

Mr. Montrose tipped his hat. "I do apologise, Mrs. Reed. Just doing my job."

Ginger half expected the bench where Miss Graves had been sitting to have been long vacated but was relieved to find the woman remained in place, waiting, her head bowed and her gaze steadily looking at her lap.

After taking the back bench, Ginger whispered, "Blasted press. I told them nothing, as I know nothing."

A shiver raced down Ginger's spine when Edith failed to respond. "Miss Graves?" Ginger whispered. "Miss Smythe?"

Ginger jumped to her feet and slid in beside the unmoving body of Miss Graves, who was slumping to her left. Even as she checked the woman's wrist for a pulse, she knew there'd be none.

Edith Smythe, was dead.

CHAPTER TWENTY-TWO

*G*inger quickly scanned the area, which was filled with everyday people lingering about. Not one person her focus landed on looked nervous or apprehensive. There were none darting away on foot as if being chased.

Perhaps that was where the murderer's brilliance lay. They blended in—casually smelling the flowers, picnicking on a blanket, or lounging in the sun.

"Ginger?"

Ginger turned to her husband's voice. "Oh good. You got my message."

"Indeed I did," he said with tight lips. "I'm delighted to see you are in one piece."

"And why shouldn't I be?"

Basil frowned, his hazel eyes latched on to the body, sitting upright on the bench. "Because of this, perhaps?" Basil gave Ginger a knowing look. "Is she?"

Ginger nodded, glancing back at the deceased. Passersby would simply assume she was resting her eyes, perhaps enjoying the park's serenity, the chirping of birds, and the children's laughter.

"I was interrupted by Mr. Montrose," Ginger explained, "and by the time I got her to her, she was already dead.

A pair of foot officers came into view, and Basil jogged to them, giving them instructions that Ginger couldn't understand but could guess. A doctor and an ambulance would be required, and Inspector Van der Meer must be notified.

Ginger made a cursory examination of the body, the best she could without drawing attention. The last thing they wanted was to create a scene or a sense of panic.

But a killer was on the loose.

Basil returned with two tall foot officers at his heels. They nodded to each other with grim expressions as they took in the body.

"Whatever it was happened fast and never aroused suspicion," Ginger said to Basil.

"It appears that she didn't fight back," Basil said. "The attacker quite likely came from behind. Are we certain she's Miss Graves' sister?"

"I don't know," Ginger answered honestly. What she did know was the corpse belonged to Edith Smythe. The telling sickle-shaped scar on her wrist confirmed it.

"Tell me again about Montrose," Basil said. "Do you believe your encounter with the man to be by chance, or could it have been a purposeful diversion?"

"Either," Ginger said, "though I'm leaning towards diversion." Was it possible that the American was a government agent as well? It felt like there were more agents at these Olympic games than athletes!

"Who could he have been working with?"

Ginger shrugged. "I wish we had a witness to tell us if a man or woman had bumped into our victim, but as you can see, people are in constant motion in this park, with hundreds milling about . . ."

"A needle in a haystack."

"Exactly."

The crowd that had gathered showed signs of being disrupted, and soon, the police officers returned with the requested attendants in tow. The ambulance men carried a stretcher whilst the pathologist came with his black bag. The situation had caught the public's attention.

Basil instructed the officers, "Keep them back."

The pathologist extended a hand to Ginger. "I'm Dr. Jansen."

"Mrs. Reed, as you seem to know already. I'm pleased to meet you."

"A pleasure, Mrs. Reed," the doctor returned. "Despite the circumstances. So, what do we have here?"

"She died in a public place, almost instantly," Ginger

said. "I wouldn't be surprised if you find another needle prick and poison in the blood."

Dr. Jansen did his duty and declared the woman dead. "Have you any idea who she is?"

"She claimed to be Nora Graves's sister," Basil said, "but we don't know that for a fact."

The doctor hummed, then surprised Ginger by removing the hat from the corpse and shocking her further by running his fingers through the dead woman's hair.

"Dr. Jansen?" Ginger asked.

"Don't be alarmed," the doctor said. "I was just confirming a suspicion. The woman shares facial features with Miss Nora Graves, but that doesn't necessarily mean they are related. Many people find they have a doppelgänger in the world with whom they have no blood relationship."

"But," Basil prompted.

"Miss Nora Graves had double hair whorls. Singular whorls aren't that common, but double ones are even more rare."

"Is that what you were looking for here?" Ginger asked.

With a nod, Dr. Jansen answered. "Yes. And have a look."

Ginger followed the path of the doctor's finger on the victim's scalp. "There's one here and one here. They're difficult to manage, but hats, scarves, and the turban now in fashion make them easier to conceal."

"Or the choice to wear pigtails?" Ginger said. Nora Graves's hairstyle on the track now made sense.

Once the body was on the stretcher, the attendants covered it with a sheet and then walked it out of the park to the ambulance.

"I'll be at the mortuary if you need me," Dr. Jansen said. "I'm certain to get a visit from Inspector Van der Meer."

"Please update him on everything you've learned here," Basil said.

Dr. Jansen tipped his hat and trotted after the ambulance men.

"I wonder if Mr. KIaassen has had another syringe go missing recently," Ginger said.

"Let's call in and find out." Basil patted his stomach. "Perhaps Scout would like to join us for lunch."

CHAPTER TWENTY-THREE

The pleasing scent of hay and horse welcomed Ginger and Basil as they entered the Olympic stables. Mr. KIaassen flashed a quick look of annoyance when he spotted them. "You know you're supposed to have special clearance to come inside here," he said.

Basil flashed his police identification card. "This is my special clearance, thanks to the Dutch police."

"Very well, I'm in a rush today." Mr. KIaassen pushed up on his spectacles. "What can I do for you?"

"Did you happen to have a second syringe go missing?" Ginger asked.

Mr. KIaassen laughed. "No, indeed. In fact, the one I thought I had lost has shown up. It seems it rolled under a trough after I used it last."

Ginger stared at Basil. *If the syringe found in the canal didn't originate from here, where did it come from?*

"You're quite certain?" Basil asked. "There's no way someone could've planted one there?"

"I'm certain, Chief Inspector. It has a scratch on the surface that would be hard to duplicate. I recognised it as one of mine immediately."

"Did you ever have the opportunity to meet Miss Nora Graves before she passed away?" Ginger asked. "Did she ever come to the stables?"

Mr. KIaassen made a face. "I don't see why she should. And no, I didn't meet her. I haven't met many athletes. I only care about the four-footed sort. Now, if you'll excuse me."

Once Mr. KIaassen was out of earshot, Ginger said, "I suppose he had means, but I fail to see motive and opportunity."

"I concur," Basil returned with a sigh. "It feels like we're taking one step forward and two steps back."

"Hopefully, Inspector Van der Meer is having more luck than we are." Ginger grabbed Basil's arm and led him along. "Let's find our son and get something to eat."

LUNCH WAS CONSUMED at another delightful outdoor eatery. Ginger, enjoying the day and especially the extra time with Scout, put aside the case that had consumed her and Basil to focus on their son.

"Honestly," Scout said between bites of his sandwich, "I feel like I've died and gone to heaven. All these horses are the cream of the crop, eh?"

"Is it so much different from what you do at school?" Scout attended a small speciality boarding school that focused on horses and horse training.

"All the brushing and feeding is the same," Scout said, "but the level of excitement is different. When a horse and rider wins, everyone is all cock-a-hoop, and when one loses, it's like the poor horse had died."

"Do you have a favourite?" Ginger asked.

"Pegasus Pride, of course. That stumble wasn't his fault."

Ginger pinched her lips, red with fresh lipstick. "You think the problem lay with Mr. Masters, do you?"

"Of course," Scout said. "The failing is always with the rider. And Mr. Masters . . ."

"What about him?" Basil asked.

"He's been distracted," Scout answered. "Perhaps he's ill. I don't know. I hope they do better in the jumping."

"We shall have to watch that, shan't we, Basil?"

"We'll do our best, love."

Ginger gave a slight nod of understanding. So long as the case didn't interfere, he'd be there.

"What do you think of Mr. KIaassen?" Ginger asked, changing the subject.

Scout shrugged. "He's a funny man. Likes animals more than people, which I understand. If I weren't a slight lad, suitable for riding, I'd think of becoming a veterinarian."

They ate companionably, and having finished her half-sandwich, Ginger discreetly held her compact mirror under the table's edge and had a quick look. Nothing like a bit of lettuce in the teeth to ruin one's smile. The sun's rays caught the glass.

"Oy, Mum!" Scout protested. "You flashed the light in my eyes."

Ginger slipped the compact back into her handbag. "Sorry, love."

A barking dog caught their attention, and Ginger smiled at the black-and-white Boston terrier on a leash. "He looks like Boss did when he was a puppy."

The little dog wasn't yet well trained and strained on his leash, reaching to sniff Scout's hand.

The owner, a bright-faced young girl in a frilly frock, her hair in pigtails and wearing flat, buckle-up shoes, said with exasperation, "Hondje, *stop*!"

"It's all right," Scout said to the girl. "He can smell my sandwich. Is it all right if I give him some ham?"

At the girl's confused look, Basil translated.

The girl smiled and nodded. "*Oké, als je wilt.*"

As Ginger watched the little dog eat the offered ham, then stare at Scout with round, hopeful eyes, she felt a sudden stab of loneliness for Boss. At least he had Ambrosia, though the dowager hadn't proved good company to the dog in the past. Ginger wondered how Ambrosia was doing alone at Hartigan House. She pictured her moping about her walking stick, making sombre taps on the marble floor. She'd be dressed in long Victoria-era skirts, her fingers heavy with large-stoned rings. Ginger had felt bad leaving her in London, but now that she and Basil were involved in two murders, it was a good thing Ambrosia had chosen to stay behind.

A rumpus snapped Ginger out of her reverie. Hondje had jerked the leash out of the girl's hand, and was running down the brick-paved street, the girl shouting, "Hondje, stop!"

She really needed to get a puppy trainer.

With bad timing, a man stepped out of the pharmacy just as Hondje was shooting by, the leash catching his feet. "Blast it, bloody mongrel!" He floundered about, trying to keep his balance, a street-side table preventing his fall. However, the bag he had in hand swooshed into the air, landing several feet from the table where Ginger sat, its contents rolling out.

One item was a syringe.

"Mr. Bottomley?"

The man in question was the annoying little journalist, whom Ginger now suspected was more than that. He snarled at her as he scooped up his belongings, bellowing, "Who does that blasted dog belong to?"

The girl and her dog had disappeared around the corner, and Ginger doubted they would see either of them again.

Basil got to his feet. "Mr. Bottomley, might I have a word?"

"Isn't it I who should be asking the questions?" Mr. Bottomley said with a huff. "I'm the newspaperman, after all."

"Are you, though?" Ginger challenged.

"We have a second murder you might be interested in," Basil said. "I'd prefer we discuss this at the police station. I'm certain Inspector Van der Meer would like to know why you need a syringe."

"I can tell you right now," Mr. Bottomley blustered. "Not that it's any of your business, but I'm diabetic."

"If that is the case, then the conversation is sure to be short," Basil said. "It will be to your advantage to cooperate with the police, Mr. Bottomley."

Begrudgingly, the man went with Basil, catching the next taxicab. In Scout's presence, Ginger was left to muse about the day's events.

"Shall we have an ice cream, Mum?"

"That's a splendid idea," Ginger said. "Then I must deliver you back to Mr. KIaassen."

CHAPTER TWENTY-FOUR

Basil accompanied Ernest Bottomley to the police station. The man's agitation was on display throughout the duration of the taxicab ride, and though Basil was secure in his belief that he could easily wrestle the stout man into submission should matters escalate, he preferred to preserve his suit.

"I tell you, you have no right," Bottomley insisted. "I have nothing to do with the athletes except to record their victories or defeats."

"Then you have nothing to worry about," Basil said. "Your full cooperation will ensure that the time you have donated to good citizenry will be minimal."

"I'm not a citizen of this country. I don't have to do anything."

Basil snorted. "I see that the spirit of the Games hasn't rubbed off on you yet."

With Basil at Bottomley's side and the foot officer

at his heels, the journalist-spy was guided through the entrance of the police station. It was good luck that Inspector Van der Meer was on the premises, as Basil didn't know how he'd be able to keep Bottomley there on just good graces. Even so, he left the man to stew by himself once delivered to the interview room.

"You found the spy," Van der Meer said after greeting Basil. "On what grounds did you bring him in?"

Basil exhaled heavily. "I fear rather thin ones, Inspector. I came upon him after he purchased a syringe from the pharmacy. He claims to be diabetic."

"What size was the syringe?"

"Not as large as the one that was dredged from the canal. Are we certain of the size of that?"

"I'm assuming there is more than one size of syringe, Chief Inspector, whether used on animals or humans. The injection mark on the body could've been made by a syringe of more than one size. As for the syringe found in the canal, the laboratory report is inconclusive. If it was used to inject poison, all evidence of such has been flushed out by canal water."

"I see," Basil said dejectedly. It would've been nice to have a small break in the case.

Van der Meer waved towards the door. "We'll have to find a way to determine if Mr. Bottomley is telling the truth about his medical situation."

"He may refuse to provide medical proof," Basil said, "but if he truly has diabetes, he'll need to give himself insulin, and he wouldn't want to bet his life on our holding him too long."

"That's a good point."

Basil followed Van der Meer into the interview room. Bottomley wasted no time in protesting.

"I demand that you release me at once!"

"Mr. Bottomley," Van der Meer said calmly. "It's not our intention to cause you distress. However, you know we are investigating not one but two murders." Sitting in one of the empty chairs, he continued, "Surely, you would desire to do what you can to help us? Especially as a reporter. Imagine the, er...what do you call it? Oh yes, imagine the dig."

"Scoop," Basil corrected with a smile.

Bottomley visibly relaxed. "Very well. So long as you know, I will write the story when I return to my room." His beady eyes darted to Basil. "Not everyone will come out smelling of roses."

"So long as you don't commit libel, Mr. Bottomley," Basil said as he took the last chair. "Now, I understand that acquiring syringes isn't easy for the common man, at least here in the Netherlands."

Van der Meer nodded. "That's true."

"One has to prove one is in the medical field unless..."

"Unless one is diabetic," Bottomley interjected. "You prove my innocence. I couldn't have purchased a syringe without my having proof of my medical condition, which I do."

The man's statement was true, but Basil didn't doubt that such a claim could be falsified, especially if one was a spy. "How many syringes have you purchased since arriving in Amsterdam?" he asked.

Bottomley hesitated.

Van der Meer prompted, "We have ways of finding this out, Mr. Bottomley. I recommend that you tell the truth."

The round cheeks of Bottomley's face bloomed crimson. "This is my third. I tell you, someone has been nicking them from me."

"You're saying your syringes have gone missing?" Basil asked.

"That's what I'm saying. At first, I thought I was losing my mind, thinking I was misplacing them, but I'm in a small hotel room. There are not a lot of places to put things. I asked housekeeping, but when I finally got them to understand me, they insisted they've not removed any of my syringes or thrown them in the rubbish bin."

"Do you have any idea who would do such a thing?"

Bottomley folded thick arms over a full chest. "My guess is Montrose."

"Jack Montrose, the American journalist?" Van der Meer asked.

"The one and the same. I saw the blighter snooping in my attaché case. I don't trust him one bit."

Basil leaned in. "Who do you work for, Mr. Bottomley?"

"You know who. *The Daily Picture.*"

Basil pressed. "No, I mean, *who* do you *work* for?"

Bottomley sniffed. "I have no idea what you mean."

Basil didn't expect a real answer. Those spy types know how to seal their lips when they want to.

Van der Meer pulled no punches. "We know that you're a government agent, Mr. Bottomley. I would presume your allegiance is with the British government, but one mustn't assume. The question for us, for me as a servant of the Dutch police, is what does a British agent or an agent working for another nation have to do with the death of two sisters?"

Bottomley stilled. "What two sisters?"

Did he truly not know about Esther Graves' death? "Miss Nora Graves and Miss Esther Graves," Basil answered. "The latter was also once known as Edith Smythe."

Bottomley's expression went blank. Basil was familiar with the look, having seen his wife adopt it on more than one occasion. The journalist offered a small shrug. "I hadn't heard, but thank you for the lead, Chief Inspector Reed, Inspector Van der Meer. I'm looking forward to writing a juicy story. Now . . ." He pushed away from the table. "Unless you plan to arrest me, I ask you to let me go on my way."

After a quick look Basil's way, Van der Meer nodded. "Thank you for your time and cooperation, Mr. Bottomley."

The man left as fast as his short legs would take

him. Once alone in the room, Basil said, "I highly doubt we'll see any such story."

"Perhaps we should follow him," Van der Meer said.

"That's already taken care of. I commissioned the officer who helped me to bring him in to tag Bottomley, underscoring the fact that it would be best if the journalist remained unaware."

Van der Meer chuckled. "I see now why you come highly recommended, Chief Inspector."

Basil couldn't help but feel pleased.

Not long afterwards, a message arrived at the police station. Mr. Bottomley had taken a taxicab to the American ship where the American contingent were staying. Twenty minutes later, he left the ship alone.

CHAPTER TWENTY-FIVE

When Ginger packed for her trip to Holland—technically speaking, it was her maid Lizzie who had packed—she had thought about bringing her hand-sized Remington Derringer pistol but had decided against it. She should have known by now to be ready for anything and to assume a situation might occur where one might be grateful for the small apparatus's influence, especially when it came to changing the mind of one with evil intent.

She could've used it now.

After delivering Scout to the stables, Ginger took a turn around the Olympic grounds. She found the usual gamut of suspects: athletes, scorekeepers, judges, journalists, and rabid fans.

She also caught sight of the American contingent, which included Miss Charlotte Hartley and Mr. Jack

Montrose, in what seemed to be an intense discussion. Their heated interchange seemed intimate and not a simple "bumping into one another" mishap like Felicia had had with Mr. Bottomley.

Mr. Montrose held the athlete's arm like he'd been used to touching her. Had the two been lovers? It wasn't beyond the realm of possibility.

In a fit of anger, Miss Hartley pulled away from Mr. Montrose's grip, leaving the man to stew, his brow deeply furrowed. He pulled down on his hat before stuffing his fists into his trouser pockets and shuffling away.

Up in the British section of the crowd, Ginger spotted Felicia and Charles sitting side by side. Ginger was delighted to see they were there and started towards the section, but Felicia stood before she could climb the stairs. The stadium was too noisy to call out and be heard, and Ginger paused in indecision. Should she join Charles, wait with him for Felicia's return, or go after Felicia?

Her sister-in-law was probably seeking the ladies' room, a prospect Ginger thought would do her good as well, so she backtracked and headed that way.

A ROW of high windows along the wall above the sinks let in strong natural light from the summer sun.

When she didn't immediately see Felicia, Ginger

assumed she was simply in one of the cubicles so took advantage of a vacant cubicle herself. Finishing, she was about to step out, still on the lookout for Felicia, but caught a glimpse of Miss Hartley entering the room. That woman certainly got around. Ginger quickly slipped back into the cubicle, stepping onto the toilet seat so her feet wouldn't give her presence away.

"Is it empty?" The accent was American, and Miss Hartley's voice.

"I think so." This voice was British and one of which Ginger had intimate knowledge. Felicia.

"Good," Miss Hartley said. "I've locked the door."

Why would Miss Hartley lock the door to the loo?

"Why have you summoned me here?" Felicia's voice again. "We shouldn't be seen together."

"Who can see us?" Miss Hartley's voice was tight with agitation. "I told you, we're alone."

"Lower your voice," Felicia returned. "The windows are open."

"She's been dispatched."

"What do you mean by 'dispatched'?" Felicia said. "You promised to deliver her to us."

"And we have."

Ginger heard the smirk in Miss Hartley's voice. "She's safely lying in the Amsterdam morgue."

Mr. Montrose did *create a diversion!* Miss Hartley was their killer!

And Felicia was very much in danger.

Using her handy compact, Ginger carefully positioned it over her head, above the cubicle ledge, to capture the image of the two women standing near the locked door. Felicia stepped closer to Charlotte Hartley.

Too close.

"You promised her alive!" Felicia said tersely.

Scoffing, Miss Hartley answered, "Well, we had a better offer if she was dead. As you know, money talks."

Oh, why hadn't Ginger brought her Remington? She had to do something.

Impulsively, she flushed the toilet.

"Who's there?" the American called.

Casually, Ginger stepped out of the cubicle. "Oh, hello, Felicia, I didn't see you there."

Felicia's shock registered across her face. Clearly, her training wasn't complete.

"Ginger?"

"Mrs. Reed?"

"I hope I haven't disturbed anything." Casually, Ginger went to the sink and washed her hands. She used her compact to apply a little powder to her nose, then turned to the two staring ladies. "Have I?"

Miss Hartley's eyes narrowed. "How much did you hear?"

"Nothing I didn't already know . . . that the police don't already know." That was only partly true. The police didn't know that Miss Hartley was the killer, only that Esther Graves was in the mortuary "But why don't you tell me what's really going on?"

"Why should I tell you anything?" Miss Hartley challenged.

Felicia gave a subtle shake of her head. "I think we've finished here anyway," she said. "Why don't we all just go and watch the Games? I'm dying to know who wins, aren't you?"

"I'm not going to die at all," Miss Hartley said. In an instant, it was clear who the more seasoned agent was. Before Felicia knew what had happened, Miss Hartley had her in a neck hold, the needle of a syringe at her neck.

Ginger swallowed hard. Felicia, her eyes as round as Ginger's compact mirror, stilled. In the past, Felicia would've whimpered, begged, or even burst into tears, but this new Felicia made a gallant effort not to give in to fear. Ginger had to give her credit for that.

"How long have you been an agent for America?" Ginger asked. She wanted Charlotte Hartley to slow down, cool her emotions, and to keep her from pressing the syringe plunger.

"Not as long as you've been an agent, Mademoiselle LaFleur!"

Ginger's eyes flashed to Felicia. The truth was about to come out, and perhaps it was time.

"Yes! I know about you," Miss Hartley continued with a chuckle. "Your reputation precedes you."

"It does, Ginger," Felicia admitted, her voice tight. "You can imagine my surprise when I learned."

"Well, you understand now why I couldn't say anything," Ginger said, her heart heavy for Felicia's plight. "It's why I was so upset when I realised you had joined."

"Oh, boo hoo!" Miss Hartley said. "This is all very heartwarming, but unfortunately, you're both bound for a sad end." Miss Hartley pressed the needle of the syringe against Felicia's bare neck.

"Wait!" Ginger said. "At least satisfy my curiosity before you 'dispatch' us. As one fellow agent to another."

Miss Hartley sniffed. "Very well, what do you want to know?"

"For starters, why kill Nora Graves and her sister Esther?"

"Oh, you *really* have been out of service for a while, haven't you, Mrs. Reed? I'm sure you know by now that Esther Graves was a double agent with Britain and Austria-Hungary during the war. You probably knew her as Edith Smythe, but her real name is Eszter Sari. Just before the war broke out, her family immigrated to England, changing their last name to Graves. Nora was a child and wouldn't remember ever living in Hungary, but Eszter, now Esther, was older and resented the move.

"Even though her loyalties remained with Hungary, Esther proved highly intelligent and opportunistic, offering herself to the British government to work in the war effort. But her motives were duplicitous. All along, she intended to spy on Britain for Austria-Hungary, a German ally. But when the war ended, she found herself on the losing side with no future in either country."

"The British agency has been after her ever since, I suppose," Ginger said as things started to fall into place. "And with her younger sister competing in the Olympics, the agency hoped to flush her out and bring her to justice. Is this assumption correct, Felicia?"

Felicia started to nod but winced at the prick of the needle at her throat. "Yes."

"That I understand," Ginger said, then addressed Charlotte Hartley. "But what concern is it of yours?"

"During her spying on *your* nation, Esther Graves came into possession of something we want back. We suspected she might show up to see her sister. Perhaps get money from her."

"What on earth did Esther Graves have that the American government would be so desperate to get back?" Ginger pressed.

Miss Hartley sneered. "As if I would tell you. Let's just say it's information that the American government doesn't want to get out."

"Why kill Nora Graves?" Ginger asked. "I'd think she would've been more profitable to you alive. Seeing that she was the lure for Esther?"

"I thought she was Esther. It was dark. I thought I'd

caught the older sister waiting for the younger. Nora Graves was collateral damage."

The compact was warm in Ginger's palm. She gave Felicia a sharp look of warning.

With a quick press of the silver button, the compact opened. Ginger faced the mirror towards the ribbon of light streaming in from the high windows, directing the bright reflection into Miss Hartley's eyes.

It was enough to blind her, even if for just a fraction of a second, and Miss Hartley shifted her weight, loosening her grip on Felicia.

Felicia's training kicked in, and she elbowed Miss Hartley in the solar plexus. Miss Hartley buckled over.

The syringe fell to the cement floor with a clank, and Ginger kicked it out of the way. Miss Hartley grabbed Ginger's ankle, and Ginger would've gone down if Felicia hadn't stepped in to block her fall and trip up Miss Hartley instead.

Before Miss Hartley could right herself, Felicia landed on her back, pinning her down. Ginger removed the violet belt of her frock as Felicia grabbed Miss Hartley's arms, then Ginger used her belt to tie Miss Hartley's wrists behind her back. She grinned at Felicia, who was flushed with the exertion. "Nice work."

Felicia smiled back. "Thank you."

Holding Miss Hartley securely, their positions now reversed, Felicia said, "I think it's time to seek out the police."

There was a pounding on the door, and a strange voice yelled, "Open up!" Then, the familiar voices of Basil and Charles called out Ginger and Felicia's names.

Ginger smiled at Felicia. "It took them long enough."

CHAPTER TWENTY-SIX

The day before, Ginger and Basil had watched the equestrian eventing. Eventing tested horse-and-rider duos in several types of riding. Today was the final event: jumping. As before, Scout wasn't going to sit with Ginger and Basil; rather, he'd be watching from across the stadium.

"Can you see him?" Ginger clutched the brim of her hat as she scanned the crowd, peering through her field glasses to the section from where the horse trainers and stable staff watched. She found Mr. Klaassen's eager face but couldn't spot Scout. Where was he?

"Scout isn't where he should be," Ginger said with a sense of worry. Scout wouldn't miss this event for the world.

"Oh, I think he is," Basil said. His lips twitched as they did when he was trying hard not to smile.

"Basil? Do you know something I don't?"

"I'm afraid you'll have to wait and see, love."

Below the grandstands was a carefully laid-out maze of hurdles of varying heights and difficulty. Many included fillers to make the jumps look more solid and intimidating, some with woodsy branches, others with flower boxes, and a few with decorative flags.

As each nation was announced and their horse and rider were presented, the crowd watched with bated breath. Would the mare or gelding make the jump, or would the rails be knocked off the supporting standards by back hooves? Would their time be quick enough to earn a medal?

Basil nudged her slightly when Pegasus Pride's name was announced. Surprised, Ginger stared at Basil.

"Miss Hughes hadn't officially removed him from the competition," he said.

"But I thought her rider had already left."

Basil smiled. "He had. Listen."

The announcer continued, "A substitution for today's event has been granted. Riding Pegasus Pride is Mr. Scout Reed."

Ginger gasped and slapped Basil's thigh. "You knew about this?"

Laughing, Basil said, "Scout had a message sent to me at the police station. He wanted to surprise you."

"Well, he most certainly has."

Ginger's heart nearly burst with pride at seeing

Scout perched on the top of the chestnut gelding, wearing Britain's colours. She held her breath as the timer started and Scout nudged Pegasus Pride towards the first hurdle.

Ginger held her breath. Scout cleared the first jump, and she breathed again. The stakes were so much higher now that her son was competing. Another hurdle. Then the next. Each one cleared with inches to spare. All the time Scout had spent with Pegasus Pride had created a bond close enough for the two to perform as one.

The next hurdle was the highest and had the most filler, enough to intimidate an experienced horse and rider. Ginger grasped her hands in silent prayer. Horse and rider approached the ground line, and Ginger tensed. Scout was airborne but safely remained in the saddle as Pegasus Pride cleared the jump and landed on the other side. The crowd applauded in appreciation.

The water jump was the final hurdle—a challenge that bested many. With her heart in her throat, she watched Scout guide Pegasus Pride to the glimmering pool. At that moment, Ginger saw not the young equestrian athlete living his Olympic dream but the young gap-toothed lad she and Boss had befriended on the SS *Rosa*, his eyes pools mixed with innocence and worldliness. Back when he'd called her Missus instead of Mum.

Time stood still as Pegasus Pride flew over the water like his winged namesake.

Applause broke out as the gelding landed, and Scout took him swiftly to the finish line.

Tears ran down Ginger's face, and she hurried to wipe under her eyes before a trail of mascara marred her cheeks.

"Brilliant!" Basil proclaimed. "Absolutely brilliant."

"Wasn't he?" Ginger said, agreeing. "Weren't they?"

The scores were announced, and Ginger gripped Basil's arm. "Did he just—?"

"I think so, love, I think so."

The event ended with the three medallists announced. "And in third place, for bronze, Scout Reed on Pegasus Pride."

GINGER COULDN'T HAVE BEEN MORE thankful for the goodness in her life. Felicia—who'd shown up at the Games just in time to see Scout's grand performance—immediately arranged a celebration party at her flat for the following evening. Despite her tendency to make Ginger a little crazy, Felicia was the best sister-friend Ginger could ever ask for. Felicia had been a child when Ginger had married her brother Daniel, Lord Gold—*oh mercy, it felt like another lifetime ago*—but now was a beautiful, sophisticated lady of stature and grace. The ten years between them felt like nothing now.

The drawing room of Felicia and Charles' flat was aglow with warm light and filled with the energy of attractive and well-dressed people. Felicia proved to be a delightful and gracious host, looking stunning in a long evening gown—midnight blue with sequins that glistened like stars when she moved.

The guests mingled with drinks in one hand and bits of cheese or nuts in the other. Louis Armstrong played on a gramophone in the corner. Chairs were along the perimeter, with space left in the centre for the dancing yet to come.

Ginger watched Basil across the room. He and Charles both wore tail-coats and were speaking about sports, drinks in their hands. As if feeling Ginger's gaze, Basil glanced over, his hazel eyes taking her in as he smiled casually. She nodded, and he lifted his glass—a silent recognition, shared admiration, and a knowing of the treasures they shared. Along with their deep mutual affection and respect, they shared a family. Baby Rosa, whom Ginger was desperate to return to London again to see, and their adopted son Scout, the Olympian!

The young man of the hour was enjoying the attention. Despite his protests, Scout wore a suit and dress shoes, his hair oiled back like the gentlemen in the room. He entertained a small crowd with his rendition of the race, the story getting grander with each retelling. Ginger chuckled. Scout had always been a bit of a ham. She lifted the skirts of her evening gown—a green satin affair with thin shoulder straps, a low back, and a long feathery hemline—thankful that Lizzie had thought to include a gown amongst her many day frocks, and joined Scout and his many admirers.

"I understand that this strapping young man belongs to you, Mrs. Reed." Inspector Van der Meer had joined the festivities with his young wife.

"Indeed, he does," Ginger said.

Mrs. Van der Meer, in strongly accented English, said, "You and the chief inspector must be very proud."

"We've always been proud of Scout," Ginger said. "And certainly, an Olympic medal is a feather in his cap. He's worked very hard to get to this point."

She shared a knowing look with Scout, who understood the words had a greater meaning. He'd also worked hard to get off the streets and join the world where Ginger belonged.

"Thanks, Mum."

Marion Hughes came late to the party. Ginger had only ever seen the woman dressed in jodhpurs, her head under unremarkable caps, so she didn't recognise her. Miss Hughes was dressed in a glamourous pink evening gown, and her bob was styled in finger curls and held in place with a gem-filled headband.

Ginger hurried to greet her. "Welcome, Miss Hughes. I'm so glad you could make it at short notice."

"Thank you. I'm not much for parties, but I've learned to be prepared for everything. The win is as much mine as it is Scout's."

"Of course, and once again, congratulations."

"Pegasus Pride would've won with Mr. Masters. It was fortuitous for your son that he'd left early."

Ginger didn't know if she agreed with Miss Hughes' brash assessment that her rider would've done better or as well as Scout.

Once the partygoers realised that Miss Hughes had joined them, they soon crowded about her to offer congratulations, the scandal surrounding her false arrest forgotten.

Still, once the more benign topics were exhausted and wine and spirits consumed, talk turned to the murders of the Graves sisters. Miss Charlotte Hartley was in the custody of the British government; however, Mr. Jack Montrose, if those were their real names, was listed as missing. As an agent of the American government, Ginger assumed he'd somehow been smuggled out of Holland.

The papers covered the murders as well, but as Ginger had expected, espionage was not mentioned. Felicia and Charles were keeping mum on the subject. "Dashed if I know anything," was all Charles would say.

As for Ernest Bottomley, it was discovered he was working for both the British and the Americans. He did have diabetes, but his syringes hadn't gone missing, he'd been handing them to Miss Hartley. As Ginger had suspected, he'd also been working with Charles and Felicia. Inspector Van der Meer had told Basil that Bottomley wasn't one of the good ones, and he'd been right. As Miss Hartley said, "money talks", and

Bottomley preferred the cash the Americans offered over the prestige granted by the British. Had he known of Ginger's alias when he approached them on the ship? If so, her reputation truly had preceded her, a thought that caused her a great sense of alarm.

Much like the very first time they'd met, Basil crossed the floor until he stood before Ginger. "Might I have this dance?"

"Certainly, Mr. Reed."

Ginger and Basil shared a laugh. She'd initially used this title with him before she'd learned of his position at Scotland Yard.

Dancing was something that both Ginger and Basil had a talent for. They began with the foxtrot, gliding as one across the dance floor, Basil leading expertly so as not to run into the other dancing couples. A collective "whoop!" was shouted when the music changed to energetic jazz, and a young Dutch couple took the floor, swinging the Lindy Hop, a popular dance named after Charles Lindbergh's New York to Paris flight the year before. Everyone moved to the rhythm of the music as they clapped to cheer the couple on. With quick steps, the couple swivelled in time to the music, their shoes sliding along the wooden floor, then ended their performance with the woman making an athletic flip over the man's back.

When they vacated the spot, Basil pulled Ginger in. Holding hands, they moved with the music, together and apart, releasing one hand to shimmy and swivel in perfect timing, the fringe on Ginger's dress snapping dramatically. Basil grabbed Ginger's waist, and she flung her legs to the right of his torso, then the left. Touching the floor again, they broke into the Charleston, snapping their legs out behind themselves.

Basil brought Ginger close, and breath heavy with the glow of the thrill of the dance, they bowed out, making room for the next couple.

"Nicely done, Mum and Dad," Scout said. His face was rosy, and he glanced away sheepishly as if he felt embarrassed but knew he shouldn't.

"Perhaps you'll take those dance lessons after all," Ginger said.

Scout shook his head. "I think I'll stick to training horses."

The evening was lovely, and Ginger couldn't think of a better way to end their time in Amsterdam. She looked for Felicia, wanting to thank her again for organising such a fabulous party at short notice.

She found Felicia, who looked serious as she read a note she held in her hand.

"Is something wrong?" Ginger asked.

"We've had a telegram." Felicia held out the note, her eyes dark with emotion. "It's from Digby."

The missive was short and to the point.

"The Dowager Lady Gold is suffering from an underdetermined malady. She wishes for her granddaughter and granddaughter-in-law to return to London."

CHAPTER TWENTY-SEVEN

Ginger, Basil, and Scout left the next morning for London, missing the Olympic closing ceremony. Ginger didn't feel even a smidgen of disappointment as she was quite ready to go home. Felicia and Charles had "things" to take care of but promised to be in London by that evening.

When the taxicab finally pulled up in front of Hartigan House, Ginger felt like sprinting through the wrought-iron fencing to the heavy wooden door as if it were its own Olympic event.

Drat it all! The door is locked. She rang the doorbell and peered through a tall window, which flanked the front door. Inside was the high ceiling from which hung the large electric chandelier, the curving staircase with its emerald-green carpet runner leading to the upper floor, and the black and white tiles of the entryway, now being quickly traversed by her serious-looking butler.

"Madam," Digby said with a shortness of breath. "Welcome home." To Basil, he nodded, "And you, sir," then to Scout, "and to you, young sir. I hear congratulations are in order."

Ginger hoped that Digby's polite enquiries at this moment meant that bad news wasn't imminent.

"Is the dowager awake?" Ginger asked as she removed her gloves and hat. "Is she in her chambers?"

"Yes, to both questions," Digby said, continuing with a note of weariness. "She's quite awake."

"And Miss Rosa?" Ginger asked.

"She's in the nursery, madam. Nanny Green recently informed me that the little girl is sleeping."

At their voices, Boss appeared at the top of the stairs. Taking a moment to stretch, he started down the stairs. Ginger hurried to greet him halfway, swooping him into her arms. "Hello, old man!" Snuggling her nose into his black-and-white fur, rather more grey than black these days, she added, "Did you miss me?"

Boss confirmed that he had by licking Ginger's cheek.

"I missed you, too, as did this spectacular young lad." Ginger handed Boss to Scout, who'd stopped on the step below her. "Why don't you take him to the kitchen, Scout? I'm sure Mrs. Beasley has a treat for both of you."

"Perhaps I'll allow you some time alone with

Ambrosia," Basil said when they reached the landing. Ambrosia's bedroom door was cracked open, and she was clearly awake and sitting in her bed. "If she were really counting down her last minutes," Basil whispered, "a doctor would be on the premises. She wants to see you, and I should check in with the Yard. Morris will want a report."

Ginger imagined the oversized and demanding superintendent would want nothing less. "Of course, love. I'll ring you if you're needed."

Basil kissed her cheek and skipped back down the steps. Ginger smoothed out her day frock, pushed her red locks behind her ears, and then, after a breath, knocked on the door.

"Grandmother?"

"Oh, Ginger, there you are. Finally!"

Ginger crossed the floor of the large room and took Ambrosia's hand. The elderly lady had a look of frailty, but her colour was good, and the glimmer in her eyes was lively.

"Grandmother." Ginger kissed the matriarch on the forehead, then took an empty chair close to the bed, which had no doubt been well used by Ambrosia's maid, Langley. "I came as soon as I could."

Ambrosia stared past Ginger at the open door. "Where's Felicia?" Her watery eyes blazed with indignation. "Don't tell me she's not coming? With me on my deathbed?"

"Grandmother!" Ginger said with sincere alarm.

"Who said you were on your deathbed?" Ambrosia didn't look like someone at death's door. "What has the doctor said?"

Ambrosia flapped a pale, veiny hand, and Ginger noticed it was free of the rings that normally adorned it. Perhaps she did have reason to worry.

"Just a bit of indigestion. Not so uncommon for someone my age."

"Then, why did you send such an alarming message?"

Ambrosia rolled her bulbous eyes. "I thought it would bring Felicia home. It appears I was wrong."

Ginger was about to admonish Ambrosia for such foolishness, not to mention, giving her a heart attack, but stopped herself when a tear escaped Ambrosia's eye. With a shaky hand, the dowager ran a finger along the folds around her eye as if to erase the evidence.

Ginger took Ambrosia's hand. "Grandmother, you're not wrong. Felicia is on her way. She had to catch the ferry after ours, but it was only a one-hour delay."

Ambrosia livened up at the news. "Well, she always was one to be fashionably late. Please ring for tea, Ginger. You can tell me all about these Olympic Games."

Ginger rang the bell, and one of the maids soon popped in. After a curtsy, she said, "Welcome home, madam."

"Thank you, Grace," Ginger said. "The dowager and

I would like tea. Bring three cups, please, as Lady Davenport-Witt will be joining us soon."

After the maid left, Ambrosia said, "I listened on the radio, you know."

Ginger arched a brow in surprise. "Is that so? I didn't think sports were of interest to you."

"It's all anyone in the house talked about. All the maids, the butlers. I had to know what the hubbub was about."

Ginger glanced out the window so Ambrosia wouldn't read the surprise on her face. That the dowager spoke to the staff about anything besides what they could do for her was stunning. "How is Pippins?" she asked. "Have you seen him about?"

"Of course I've seen him about. You don't expect him to stay in the attic, do you? He and your dog spend a lot of time in the back garden. I can hardly miss seeing them if I'm to get a breath of fresh air."

The tea arrived, and Ginger prepared a cup for them both, handing Ambrosia hers first. "What did the doctor *really* say?"

Ambrosia blinked her round eyes slowly. "I've already told you."

"Indigestion, I know. But you're still in bed, Grandmother. Is there something else?"

Ambrosia huffed. "Oh, I might as well tell you, as you've got a way of finding things out anyway. The doctor thinks I have a weak heart. Oh, don't look so forlorn. Everyone has to die someday. And he said I still have quite a few good months left. With my stubbornness, perhaps years."

Ginger bit back a smile. "The doctor actually said that?"

"Yes. Such cheek. Now, tell me about that lad of yours. Did he really win something?"

"He did!" Ginger was happy to tell Ambrosia all about Scout's unexpected opportunity and described the stadium and the energy of the crowd as best as she could. Ambrosia, to Ginger's astonishment, seemed sincerely interested. By the time Ginger ended the retelling, Felicia had arrived.

"Grandmama! You scared me to death," Felicia said as she greeted her grandmother. "And here you are chatting away, enjoying tea."

"And there's a cup for you," Ambrosia said. Her blue eyes peeked through papery folds of skin and took in Felicia like a thirsty person finding water. "Look at you, my dear. I've missed you."

"I've missed you too, Grandmama."

Ginger gave up her seat for Felicia; for the first time, she saw the resemblance between the two Gold ladies. Beyond the similar profile was a fire for life, a determination of spirit, and an unwillingness to give up or give in. Though they'd faced differing challenges in their respective generations, their approach to difficulties and to going after what they wanted in life was much the same. "You have a lot to catch up on," Ginger said with a soft smile, "so I'll leave the two of you to it. I'm desperate to see Rosa."

CHARLES HAD WARNED Felicia that she must make sacrifices to join the secret service. Felicia wondered now if she'd been too hasty. In that decision-making moment, she'd only wanted to alleviate the deep pain she'd felt on what looked like the imminent demise of her marriage and the despair that came with the sense that her life had no meaning. Now, here with her ailing grandmother, she doubted her life choice.

Though they'd rushed back to London spurred on by Grandmama's missive, Charles had been instructed to report to the "office" as soon as they arrived. When one gave one's life to serve one's country, one gave away one's freedoms, such as how one spent one's time and where one spent it.

Their mission, their *failed* mission, in Amsterdam was over. They, along with that loathsome Bottomley, were supposed to flush out "Esther Graves" and bring her back to England to be charged with war crimes. They had not only failed to bring her in, but they'd also failed at keeping her alive. One American agent had disappeared in the way only secret agents could. Probably with a new identity, as no one with his name and description had been picked up at the seaports or airports in Holland. Felicia had wanted a win. Especially for her first mission. She wanted to prove to everyone, especially herself, that she was cut out for this. Charles had kindly reassured her that many missions were unsuccessful, and this wasn't likely the last one.

Her husband would return home with news, and Felicia wondered where they'd be sent to next. Charles thought Africa or perhaps India. Felicia hoped for something much closer to home.

"Felicia?"

"Yes, Grandmama."

"What are you daydreaming about?"

"Oh, nothing." Felicia held her grandmother's bony hand. "I'm just glad to be here with you. You're looking much better than I'd anticipated."

"The ability to bounce back quickly is a trait we Gold ladies share. Just seeing you has restored my vitality. I hope you'll be staying now that you're home."

Felicia wouldn't say that their stay in London was probably temporary. That was news she'd save for another day. "I'm here now, Grandmama. That's what matters."

CHAPTER TWENTY-EIGHT

Basil, with his usual energy, strolled through the entrance of Scotland Yard. Composed of two red-brick buildings, each with decorative bands of white limestone, the police station faced the Victoria Embankment. Basil briefly thought that he preferred the murky waters of the Thames to the myriad of canals in the Netherlands.

"Welcome back, Chief Inspector!"

Basil turned to the friendly voice belonging to Constable Braxton. The young officer had worked closely at Basil's side for years now, and Basil wondered if he was due a promotion. Perhaps they were both due a promotion.

Braxton continued, "It wasn't much of a holiday, I hear. Your blackmailer is waiting in the interrogation room."

Basil stopped in his tracks. "My blackmailer?"

"Yes, sir. A Mr. Bernard Masters was picked up at the ferry terminal on your instructions."

"So, they got him? Bravo."

"Yes, sir. Here's a file with the information you requested."

Basil had sent the Yard a telegram informing the force about Bernard Masters' return to England, his suspected crimes, and the request for other information regarding the man. He picked up his pace, eager to face the unscrupulous jockey. Before he got to the interrogation room, Morris stepped into the corridor. "Good timing, Reed." He coughed into his fist. "I was about to have him locked up, awaiting your return. I don't think I could hold him more than a day."

"Probably not," Basil said. "Has he confessed to anything?"

"No." More coughing ensued, and Basil felt a twinge of concern. On closer look, the superintendent looked pale, and had he lost weight?

Morris continued, "Bad news, he's asked for a solicitor."

"I suppose that's to be expected."

Morris broke into a fit of coughing. "I need some water. I'll meet you in there."

Basil watched the man until he disappeared around the corner, then headed for the interrogation room. There, he found a disgruntled Bernard Masters sitting beside his stone-faced solicitor.

"Hello again, Mr. Masters," Basil said. Introductions

were exchanged with the solicitor, and then Basil took a seat. "Let's jump right in," he said. "You've been arrested for alleged blackmail."

Masters' expression twisted with barely suppressed rage. "I deny everything."

"You deny taking money from Miss Nora Graves, Mr. KIaassen, and your employer Miss Hughes, among others, in return for your silence."

"I do."

Basil groaned inwardly. It would be too much to expect cooperation and a full confession. "You must be aware that we've looked into your finances." Basil opened the file Braxton had given to him.

"Every week, you make regular deposits into your bank account like clockwork." Basil concealed the contents of his file as he read. "Twelve pounds every Monday. Twenty-three on Tuesdays. Fifty on Wednesdays . . ." He looked up. "You understand what I'm getting at?"

"So what?" Masters snorted. "Being organised and consistent in one's personal affairs isn't a crime."

"No, but blackmail is." Basil dropped the accounting notebook Scout had found on the table with dramatic flair. "This book documents figures and initials, the exact figures and initials recorded with, as you say, organisation and consistency. GC, Gerrit KIaassen, has admitted to paying you to keep his secret—apparently to do with a horse that died suddenly while in his care. And MH, Marion Hughes? She revealed the secret you were holding over her head because she'd rather a stranger like me know than be beholden to someone like you, whom she thought she could trust.

"She told you?"

The solicitor shot Masters a look of reproach. "Mr. Masters!"

Basil smiled. It was the jockey's first crack. "Told me what, Mr. Masters?"

Masters folded his arms across his chest, his expression tense.

"Yes, she told me," Basil said, though it wasn't the whole truth. Miss Hughes had admitted to being blackmailed by her former rider but wouldn't reveal the reason for her shame. "And then there's NG, Nora Graves. What did she have to hide? Her affair with Mr. Dankworth? That was pretty much common knowledge at this point. Was that why she refused to pay?"

Masters snarled. "You'll have to ask her."

The solicitor rolled his eyes.

"Well, you know I can't do that, don't you, Mr. Masters? You're just lucky that her killers have been identified, or you would've found yourself on the top of the list. As it is, I have you for blackmail." Basil collected his file as he got to his feet. "You can say goodbye to your career as a jockey."

After a quick stop at his office, Basil felt suddenly exhausted. Paperwork could wait.

. . .

Rosa was waking just as Ginger entered the nursery. Her toddler daughter, with dark curls and rosy cheeks, grabbed the bars of her crib and pulled herself into a standing position. "Mama."

Ginger swung her little girl into the air and embraced her. "Rosa, my love!" Kissing her warm cheeks, Ginger continued. "I missed you."

"Mama," Rosa said again.

Ginger wondered about her daughter's future, what was to come, what kind of life she'd have. Would she want a career or motherhood? Could she have both? Would she travel and have adventures? Would she fall in love?

Nanny Green stepped in from her adjoining room. "Good afternoon, Mrs. Reed."

"Everything went well while I was gone, I presume?" Ginger asked though the answer was obvious.

"Yes, madam."

Ginger kissed Rosa's head. "Shall we go to the kitchen? Perhaps the cook has a biscuit for you too."

With Rosa on her hip, Ginger headed down the corridor to the staircase but paused at the open door of Ambrosia's bedroom. She took a moment to watch the two animated Gold ladies, two generations between them. One was holding on as hard as she could to the Victorian ways she'd always known, and the other, like Ginger, was hoping for a better, equal life for women and did what she could to break down the barriers.

"Rosa, the baton will be passed on to you one day. But until then, my love, I'll run the race with you."

Ginger heard voices from the sitting room as she stepped into the hall and shifted Rosa to her other hip. "Who could that be? It sounds like Daddy!"

The door had been left open, and Ginger saw the two favourite men in her life sitting across a table from each other, staring thoughtfully at an assembly of chess pieces on a chequered board.

"Basil? I thought you'd left for the Yard."

Basil got to his feet, approaching with his arms extended. "I've been and come back again." He reached for Rosa, and Ginger lifted her into his arms. "I needed to see my baby," he continued. "Isn't that right, Rosa? How is my little girl?" He kissed her head, and Ginger and Scout shared a smile.

Rosa beamed at her father. "Dada."

"Who's winning?" Ginger asked as she sauntered to the table near the fireplace where the game was taking place.

Scout grinned smugly. "Me."

Basil blew a raspberry. "I'm letting you win."

"No, you're not!" Laughing, Scout added, "I'm three moves away from checkmate."

Basil clicked his tongue. "Then Rosa came to rescue me just in time." He spun Rosa around, she giggled, and he sat her on the Turkish carpet.

Digby entered. He was a competent, if dull addition to the Hartigan House staff, who, because of a shared history with Pippins, didn't mind the unorthodox situation where a former butler remained on the premises with the new one. "Welcome home," he said. "The kitchen would like to know if you'd care for tea and biscuits."

"They're delicious biscuits," Scout said. "I've had three already."

Ginger was about to say no, but Basil said, "That would be welcome, Digby. Thank you."

Shortly afterward, Lizzie came with a tray. A delightful sprite of a girl with a narrow pixie face, she approached with a smile. After a quick curtsy, she said, "Welcome back. I hear you had an exciting time at the Olympics." Seeing Rosa, she settled the tray with the tea on the side table out of the little girl's reach. "It was very exciting listening on the wireless. I can't imagine how it must've felt to be there in person."

"It was exhilarating," Ginger said. "Especially towards the end."

"Is there anything else you need, Madam? Would you like me to unpack for you?"

"That would be appreciated," Ginger said.

Lizzie often stepped in as a lady's maid for Ginger, and Ginger had grown fond of her over the years. "Thank you, Lizzie."

"Want a biscuit, Rosa?" Scout said as he plucked a gingersnap—one of Mrs. Beasley's specialities—off a tray on the side table and held it out.

In a most adorable way, Rosa toddled over to her

older brother and took the biscuit. Ginger nearly bubbled over with joy.

The wireless played softly in the background, and when the introductory notes of a popular song came on, Ginger strolled to the large apparatus on the floor beside the window and turned up the volume.

Basil approached and took her hand as smooth notes of "The Man I Love" filled the room.

With his arm around her waist, Basil led her gently about the room. "I feel this song is apropos," Ginger said.

Basil whispered in her ear. "And I love you too, Ginger. More than you can ever know."

The song was followed by the delightful piano jazz number "Ain't Misbehaving." Scout scooped up Rosa and joined in with the dancing, and at that moment, Ginger couldn't imagine ever being happier.

CHAPTER TWENTY-NINE

*P*ippins could recall his entire life. His boyhood spent on a farm, and his wife Daisy—such a beauty and gone far too soon. The terrible war years and time spent working for, what was her name again? A Hartigan cousin. And the mistress' return to London. How long had it been now? This was where things got foggy for him. Where had that Digby fellow come from?

He was surprised by the knock on his door. If there was one thing he did remember, it was that no one ever knocked on his door.

"Pips?"

Pippins rose from the lone chair at his desk, as quickly as his old body would allow. "Madam? You should've rung."

Mrs. Reed—such a pretty lady—stepped inside and Pippins glanced about his humble quarters.

"I'm so sorry to disturb you, Pippins," Mrs. Reed began, "but I've got a proposition for you."

"Yes, madam," Pippins said.

"I know it's a lot to ask, but I'm hoping you'd consider working for Lady Davenport-Witt. Her butler, well, he had to leave, and she's desperate for someone to take his place."

Pippins squinted in confusion. "But what about you, madam?"

"Digby is here, so we'll manage. And it's only across the cul-de-sac. We'll be neighbours. I'll come to visit you every day when I can."

"Oh, I see." Pippins did see, but he was confused by a sudden flood of emotion. Sadness? Regret? He didn't know. But pleasing the mistress, that was what mattered. "Yes, helping your lady friend would be the right thing to do."

The mistress held out her arm. "Shall we go together, then?"

"What about my things?"

"I'll have Digby bring them over. Lady Davenport-Witt has a nice room for you off the kitchen. No more stairs. Won't that be nice?"

"That would be very nice, madam," Pippins said.

He followed the mistress down the stairs, gripping the rail tightly as he went. Outside, they were greeted with a lovely warm, scented breeze. A lovely day.

They walked together across the cul-de-sac and to

the back of the house, and a maid opened the door for them.

"This is Daphne," Lady Gold said. "She's going to show you around and get you acquainted with your new home."

"Yes," Pippins said. "If it pleases you, Lady Gold, I must see the state of the butler's pantry at once."

"Of course." Lady Gold hesitated, her green eyes growing damp. Like his had of late.

"Perhaps we should say goodbye," Pippins said. "For now."

Lady Gold pushed away a tear as she smiled, and Pippins smiled back. Such a lovely lady.

"Yes, Pippins," she said. "Goodbye for now."

If you enjoyed reading *Murder at the Olympics* please help others enjoy it too.

Recommend it: Help others find the book by recommending it to friends, readers' groups, discussion boards and by **suggesting it to your local library.**

Review it: Please tell other readers why you liked this book by reviewing it on Amazon or Goodreads.

* No spoilers please *

Don't miss the next Higgins & Hawke Mystery!

DEATH AT KING'S CHAPEL

Death is so cryptic!

In 1932, Boston's chief medical examiner, Dr. Haley Higgins is called to view bones at the crypt at King's Chapel and King's Chapel Burying Ground. Finding old bones in a crypt isn't unusual, but finding new bones is! Together with her good friend and investigative journalist Samantha Hawke and in co-operation with the police, Haley works to unravel the mystery behind the lost soul abandoned in the crypt. Who was the victim and why was the body left in the crypt?

Suspects range from caretakers at King's Chapel, to members of the Freedom Trail historical society, to local government officials.

As the mystery unravels, it's clear to Haley that they're dealing with a sinister mind and a culprit who wouldn't stop at killing again.

Find it on Amazon

WHAT'S NEXT

Don't miss the next Higgins & Hawke Mystery!

DEATH AT KING'S CHAPEL

Death is so cryptic!

In 1932, Boston's chief medical examiner, Dr. Haley Higgins is called to view bones at the crypt at King's Chapel and King's Chapel Burying Ground. Finding old bones in a crypt isn't unusual, but finding new bones is! Together with her good friend and investigative journalist Samantha Hawke and in co-operation with the police, Haley works to unravel the mystery behind the lost soul abandoned in the crypt. Who was the victim and why was the body left in the crypt?

Suspects range from caretakers at King's Chapel, to members of the Freedom Trail historical society, to local government officials.

As the mystery unravels, it's clear to Haley that they're dealing with a sinister mind and a culprit who wouldn't stop at killing again.

Find it on Amazon

ABOUT THE AUTHOR

Lee Strauss is a USA TODAY bestselling author of The Ginger Gold Mysteries series, The Higgins & Hawke Mystery series, The Rosa Reed Mystery series (cozy historical mysteries), A Nursery Rhyme Mystery series (mystery suspense), The Light & Love series (sweet romance), The Clockwise Collection (YA time travel romance), and young adult historical fiction with over a million books read. She has titles published in German and French, and a growing audio library.

When Lee's not writing or reading she likes to cycle, hike, and stare at the ocean. She loves to drink caffè lattes and red wines in exotic places, and eat dark chocolate anywhere.

For more info on books by Lee Strauss and her social media links, visit leestraussbooks.com. To make sure you don't miss the next new release, be sure to sign up for her readers' list!

Discuss the books, ask questions, share your opinions. Fun giveaways! Join the Lee Strauss Readers' Group on Facebook for more info.

Did you know you can follow your favourite authors on Bookbub? If you subscribe to Bookbub — (and if you don't, why don't you? - They'll send you daily emails alerting you to sales and new releases on just the kind of books you like to read!) — follow me to make sure you don't miss the next Ginger Gold Mystery!

Find me on Pinterest

www.leestraussbooks.com
leestraussbooks@gmail.com

MORE FROM LEE STRAUSS

On AMAZON

GINGER GOLD MYSTERY SERIES (cozy 1920s historical)

Cozy. Charming. Filled with Bright Young Things. This Jazz Age murder mystery will entertain and delight you with its 1920s flair and pizzazz!

Murder on the SS Rosa

Murder at Hartigan House

Murder at Bray Manor

Murder at Feathers & Flair

Murder at the Mortuary

Murder at Kensington Gardens

Murder at St. George's Church

The Wedding of Ginger & Basil

Murder Aboard the Flying Scotsman

Murder at the Boat Club

Murder on Eaton Square

Murder by Plum Pudding

Murder on Fleet Street

Murder at Brighton Beach

Murder in Hyde Park

Murder at the Royal Albert Hall

Murder in Belgravia

Murder on Mallowan Court

Murder at the Savoy

Murder at the Circus

Murder in France

Murder at Yuletide

Murder at Madame Tussauds

Murder at St. Paul's Cathedral

Murder at the Olympics

LADY GOLD INVESTIGATES (Ginger Gold companion short stories)

Volume 1

Volume 2

Volume 3

Volume 4

Volume 5

HIGGINS & HAWKE MYSTERY SERIES (cozy 1930s historical)

The 1930s meets Rizzoli & Isles in this friendship depression era cozy mystery series.

Death at the Tavern

Death on the Tower

Death on Hanover

Death by Dancing

Death on Tremont Row

Death at King's Chapel

THE ROSA REED MYSTERIES

(1950s cozy historical)

Murder at High Tide

Murder on the Boardwalk

Murder at the Bomb Shelter

Murder on Location

Murder and Rock 'n Roll

Murder at the Races

Murder at the Dude Ranch

Murder in London

Murder at the Fiesta

Murder at the Weddings

A NURSERY RHYME MYSTERY SERIES(mystery/sci fi)

Marlow finds himself teamed up with intelligent and savvy Sage Farrell, a girl so far out of his league he feels blinded in her presence - literally - damned glasses! Together they work to find the identity of @gingerbreadman. Can they stop the killer before he strikes again?

Gingerbread Man

Life Is but a Dream

Hickory Dickory Dock

Twinkle Little Star

LIGHT & LOVE (sweet romance)

Set in the dazzling charm of Europe, follow Katja, Gabriella, Eva, Anna and Belle as they find strength, hope and love.

Love Song

Your Love is Sweet

In Light of Us

Lying in Starlight

PLAYING WITH MATCHES (WW2 history/romance)

A sobering but hopeful journey about how one young German boy copes with the war and propaganda. Based on true events.

A Piece of Blue String (companion short story)

THE CLOCKWISE COLLECTION (YA time travel romance)

Casey Donovan has issues: hair, height and uncontrollable trips to the 19th century! And now this ~ she's accidentally taken Nate Mackenzie, the cutest boy in the school, back in time. Awkward.

Clockwise

Clockwiser

Like Clockwork

Counter Clockwise

Clockwork Crazy

Clocked (companion novella)

<u>Standalones</u>

Seaweed

Love, Tink

ACKNOWLEDGMENTS

They say it takes a village to raise a child, and the same is true for a book baby. I couldn't do this without the support of my husband Norm who works by my side daily, and my sons Joel and Jordan who do a lot of the heavy administration lifting.

A huge thanks to my editorial team: Angelika Offenwanger, Robbi Bryant, and Heather Belleguelle. These books wouldn't be nearly as good without your insights and finesse.

I'd also like to thank all terrific readers who love Ginger Gold as much as I do. Special shout out to Nora Graves for allowing me to use her cool name for a character in this book.